July 1ST, 1863

It is but noonday, and we can hear it from the backyard, rolling clear like summer thunder across the treetops and cornfield.

Cannon fire. Gunfire, echoing north from Gettysburg. We can see the rise of grey smoke, and know a battle has ensued.

We were certain the Rebels were gone for good when they left on the 27th. We were certain that fate would not bring them back our way. But certainty is a foolish concept, I'm learning, an idea swept away as easily as a leaf on the waters of Rock Creek.

I only pray the battle is quick and done within a day. I can only thank God that Stephen is in Maryland.

—Susanne Annalee Blackburn

Tor Books by Elizabeth Massie

Young Founders #1: 1870: Not With our Blood
Young Founders #2: 1609: Winter of the Dead
Young Founders #3: 1776: Son of Liberty
Young Founders #4: 1863: A House Divided

YOUNG FOUNDERS

1863:

A HOUSE DIVIDED

A Novel of the Civil War

Elizabeth Massie

TOR®
A TOM DOHERTY ASSOCIATES BOOK
NEW YORK

This is a work of fiction. All the characters and events portrayed in this book are either products of the author's imagination or are used fictitiously.

YOUNG FOUNDERS #4: 1863: A HOUSE DIVIDED

A Tor Book
Published by Tom Doherty Associates, LLC
175 Fifth Avenue
New York, NY 10010

www.tor.com

ISBN 0-765-35272-9
EAN 978-0765-35272-9

First Tor Digest edition: September 2004

Printed in the United States of America

0 9 8 7 6 5 4 3 2 1

To Stephen Mark Rainey, whose invaluable help and knowledge made this book possible. Thanks for everything!

To my cousin Sue Malcolm, who was a wonderful "research partner" in the fine town of Gettysburg. Next time, I'll tune up the van first!

Introduction

FOLLOWING THE END of the American Revolution in 1781, America grew as a nation. The people who populated this new country settled down to life and to the business of running it. The nation was composed of three large and unique sections—the North, the South, and the sprawling, untamed West. Each section had a different type of economy. Industry and finance dominated the North. The South depended on farming and the production of crops such as cotton, tobacco, and sugar, much of which was exported to Europe. The West also had an agricultural society, but it grew a wider variety of crops than the South and sold most of its products to the North.

During the 1850's there was almost constant quarreling between the sections. All three wanted specific things to benefit themselves. The North wanted national legislation to create a tariff to protect its industries. The West wanted legislation to provide free farms for new settlers as well as federal aid for roads and other improvements. The South wanted, basically, to be left alone. Both the North and the West believed in an expanding economy and in progressive ideas. These beliefs set these two sections apart from the more conservative South. The South resisted measures which they thought would strengthen the national government. Slavery was a Southern institution that was both economic and political, yet the North opposed it.

After the Louisiana Purchase—which more than doubled the size of the United States—bitter resentments between North and South over the slavery issue threatened to tear the nation apart. In 1820 Henry Clay of Kentucky brokered a deal known as the Missouri Compromise, which basically divided the country—north and south—into two roughly equal halves; territories seeking statehood above the line would be admitted as free states; territories below the line would be slave states.

The uneasy truce lasted thirty years. But after the United States concluded the Mexican War, disagreements about how the new territory would be apportioned again threatened to plunge the nation into war. Clay again negotiated a settlement that basically superceded the Missouri Compromise, and allowed the Mexican territories to be settled by slaveholders *and* non-slaveholders. Neither side was satisfied. The South, however, won a critical triumph with the passage of the Fugitive Slave Law, which required that runaway slaves be returned to their masters. This law would help galvanize abolitionist activities in the North.

In 1854 Illinois Senator Stephen Douglas—needing Southern support for a vast internal improvement plan—steered through Congress the Kansas-Nebraska Act. It basically invalidated the Missouri Compromise. From now on, new territories would decide for themselves whether they wanted to be admitted to the Union as a slave state or no. Fighting among rival factions in the Kansas Territory broke out almost immediately and lasted for several bloody years.

For the South the final blow came with the election of the Republican Abraham Lincoln of Illinois in 1860. Outraged, the eleven slaveholding states voted to secede from the Union and created their own country, the Confederate States of America. They elected their own president, Jefferson Davis of Mississippi.

On April 12 Confederate cannons began a bombardment of a federal arsenal at Fort Sumter in South Carolina. The fort surrendered a short time later.

The Civil War—the bloodiest event in American history—had begun.

Men and boys in the South joined up, donning the uniform of the gray, to show the rest of the United States that they couldn't be pushed around. Men and boys of the North joined up, donning the uniform of the blue, to teach the Southern rebels a good, hard lesson. Young men were especially intrigued, never having experienced a war as some of their grandfathers might have in 1812; it seemed like an adventure of glory, valor, and excitement. Although the minimum age for enlistment in the Union Army was eighteen, there is no question that many young men under that age did indeed serve. Some lied about their ages to enlist. Others had parents sign a note swearing they were of age. Others, not wanting to tell an untruth to the government representatives at the enlistment table, would write the number "eighteen" on a piece of paper and place it in their shoes. Then when asked their age, they could honestly say, "Sir, I am over eighteen."

Stephen Blackburn represents many of the young men who joined the Union Army to escape troubles at home and to prove he was a man. He longed for adventure and victory. He was like others who clamored to hold the rifle, to bear the name of soldier proudly, and to do his duty for his officers and his country. He did not know the truth of war—the ghastly wounds, the stink of death, the disease, and the expressions of fear and shock in the eyes of the men his own weapon would bring down. He did not know what it would really require of him.

Susanne Blackburn was not unlike many other young

women left behind on the home front when their brothers and fathers and uncles went off to war during the time of the "House Divided." She did her duties at home, offering aid to the war effort, anxious and angry that she was left with little information on her brother's fate, and wielding no power at all over this great and mysterious event that had lured her brother away.

These two characters, citizens of Adams County, Pennsylvania, found their lives altered irrevocably by the incidents which brought the two warring armies—the Union and the Confederates—to their own backyard to engage in one of the bloodiest and momentous clashes in American history. The clash which altered the direction of the war and the fate of the entire country: the Battle of Gettysburg.

1

April 28, 1863

I won the race, there is no doubt about it! My horse Molly and I, up Harrisburg Road from Gettysburg and then across the field to our farm we galloped, a good twelve yards ahead of Stephen and his nag most of the time. I lost my hat as we jumped the ditch by the crooked pine, but I can retrieve it in the morning. I would not stop for a hat when having a win was so close at hand!

Stephen did pull up beside me as we reached the orchard, and for a moment, as I leaned into Molly's sorrel mane and shouted, "Go girl!" I could see them beside me, neck and neck we were, with Stephen grinning his triumphant grin and his horse straining at the bit and foaming at the neck. The three deer hides we'd retrieved from the tannery in town were tied to his saddle, and flapped behind him like the wings of an enormous and furious bird. Stephen shouted, "I've got it!" But then at the last moment, when we were to pass the finish, which is always the hooded well, Stephen's horse crashed beneath an apple tree and Stephen was off. Dropping like a stone he was, and bouncing on the ground, crying out even as he struck the dirt, "I won! I passed the well first!"

He did not win. I say one must stay astride to win even if, perhaps and only perhaps, one might have been a hairs breadth ahead before he took his tumble.

We curried our horses in the barn, and gave them an extra hand of grain and extra minutes of grooming for their racing, then took the leathers inside the house to show Uncle Silas. Uncle Silas is actually my Great-uncle Silas Preston. He is seventy-three years old and has been abed for many years with a rash of infirmities from gout to asthma to dropsy. From his bed in the parlor by the fireplace he pawed the three deer hides Stephen held out for his inspection, then said, "I suppose the tanner did what he could with these pitiful specimens. Next time, Stephen, hunt like a man. Go after the full-grown animals and not the babes."

Stephen huffed, and took the hides to the kitchen. Uncle Silas is always criticizing Stephen, and often criticizing me. The tanner, Mr. Bowler, did a nice job with those hides. And I know they came from three good-sized does.

Our Great-aunt Darcy was in the kitchen, darning a pair of her stockings at the small table. She is our father's mother's sister, seventy-one years of age and not infirm as is Uncle Silas, but in her own way is limited. She smiled at the hides and said they were nice, then her eyes grew narrow and she asked, "You did not hunt them from Pratt's Woods?" No, Stephen assured her, he had not hunted the deer there, for Pratt's Woods, the small acreage of trees on the west side of the farm, contains a spirit who haunts Aunt Darcy mercilessly, so she claims.

With a little help from Aunt Darcy, I fixed supper for the four of us in the Dutch oven out in the backyard, for it is too hot to cook in the kitchen on most spring days, and we don't have a cookstove in the cellar as many neighbors do. I boiled the peas I had shelled in the morning and the sweet potatoes from the cellar, as well as a leg roast from one of the does Stephen had gutted and put in the smokehouse. When we were finished with our supper, I then took scraps to the pigs in the pen by the barn.

I wish I had a dog to eat scraps under the table at dinner. When Stephen and I lived in Rhode Island with our parents, we had a dog. His name was Tommy. Tommy could sit up, roll over on command, and sleep at the foot of my bed. Uncle Silas says dogs are a nuisance, for they chase cows and cows chased by dogs give no milk. I say pah to that! One time when I was mad at Uncle Silas I chased the cows myself and swore a fox did it.

The cows still gave milk, anyway.

I received a letter today. When Stephen and I were in town we stopped by the post office and found there was mail. A letter for Aunt Darcy from her daughter, Rudine, who lives in New Jersey with her husband and son, and a letter for me from my friend Marjorie Olson who went to Pittsburgh in March to work at the Allegheny Munitions Factory. Marjorie wrote that work is long and hard, but she lives in a boarding house with other girls and has made new friends. "Our army is in so great a need of ammunition," her letter said, "with the war against the Southerners having gone on a full two years now. You should come join me, Susie, and make your own money while helping our good men save the Union. I earn nine dollars a week! Surely you should not find yourself missing your aunt and uncle, whom I know drive you to distraction."

But I shall not go to Pittsburgh to work. I shall not leave this farm. Regardless of how difficult it is, living with a curmudgeon and mild-mannered lunatic. I will bear with it, for someday this farm will belong to Stephen and me. I am quite plain in appearance, and scarred on my arms from the fire which claimed my parents. I shall not make my way in this world by my looks, Uncle Silas has told me so, and on this one matter I am afraid he is right. I must, then, be strong and stay put. There are times when I cry, but I don't let anyone see. It would do no good, and would only make me feel worse.

When our home burned in Rhode Island, and our beautiful sweet mother and gentle father with it, I thought we should go to the charity of the church, and then to some family we did not know for servitude. But word reached Gettysburg, and we were sent for, and have lived with our great-aunt and great-uncle ever since. We were twelve when our parents burned to death. We are now sixteen. A long four years it has been. Yet I will stay strong. I will stay put.

Stephen received no letter today, but snatched up a copy of the Daily Gazette *from the druggist to read about the on-going war. He has on occasion said he would like to help put the Southerners in their place, but I'm sure he would not really go to battle. First of all, he is not old enough. Second of all, he knows I need him here. Uncle Silas grew up in South Carolina. I think when Stephen gets angry with Uncle Silas he likes to imagine that he could face a whole line of South Carolinians with a rifle and chase them clear to the Gulf of Mexico. But I do not think Stephen would enlist, for what would I do then?*

Aunt Darcy is coming upstairs now, huffing and puffing with her age. I will blow out the candle and feign sleep.

—Susanne Annalee Blackburn

2

April 28, 1863

I wonder if I shall ever understand women. Or girls, *as the case may be. I have never heard such a noise as came from Susanne when I insisted that I won our little race. And I did. It doesn't matter that I was thrown. I passed the well first. What she doesn't know is I held back and let her get a lead on me just so I could show her what Fury can do when I let him have full rein. If I'd kicked Fury from the start, I'd have been home, finishing up my supper by the time she crossed the finish.*

Susanne can get temperamental, though. No matter. Next time, I'll just let Fury go full at it and Susanne can complain all she wants to.

Talk about temperamental. Aunt Darcy went to whining about a ghostly light she thought she'd seen tonight while holding the kitchen door open for me as I came in with the well water. She whimpered and spun about, knocking the bucket and spilling the water on the floor. She worried aloud all evening, glancing frequently out the kitchen window at Pratt's Woods and wringing her wrinkled hands. How can an old woman like her be so foolish? I've hunted down in Pratt's Woods many times, and it's a right-friendly place, with nothing more evil than a few snakes and skunks. Of course I can't tell Aunt Darcy that's where I was hunting or she might up and shed her skin. And if I mention it to Uncle Silas, he'll blab it to Darcy just to amuse himself. And then she'll shed her skin.

My aunt and uncle are such vexations! Why must Uncle Silas constantly complain about what I do? Those hides were perfect. I don't think the old man has ever given me a kind word since we moved here four years ago. I wish somehow, amid all his other infirmities, he would be struck dumb. I keep this place from falling apart, I tend what little crops we've got, I take care of the horses, I chop the wood, I mend the fences, the barn, and even the creaking floors of this old weatherboard farmhouse, yet all he does is complain. If it weren't for me, they'd probably be in the Alms House right now, both of them. But maybe Aunt Darcy would like that. She'd be well away from that silly ghost that causes her such grief.

These are terrible thoughts and I'm sorry I have them. I'm sure my father would not have approved. But I can't help how I feel.

I hear Alvin Collins has gone and joined the army. And not just the army, but the cavalry! I'm told they have fabulous horses. What an exciting life that must be, charging the Rebels on horseback, everyone with sabers and rifles, and our flag flying high. It would make me proud to go off like that. There I could be a man. Here I'll always be a boy. I think the way I'm treated is hardly better than being a slave. Isn't that what the fight is about anyway?

It's no wonder Uncle Silas thinks the Rebels have the right to make their own country. I remember the fit of temper he had when President Lincoln issued the Emancipation Proclamation. He snarled and complained so hard he nearly rolled out of bed. Uncle Silas talks like the South is fighting for their rights like the founding fathers did against England in the Revolution. I guess he thinks it's fine for people with power to own other people, and maybe that's the way he feels about me and Susanne. We're like property to him, just here to see to their needs and never mind about our own. It makes me so angry that maybe I will *just join up and go into the cavalry.*

I bet Marshall and I could both pass for old enough to enlist. Last year, neither one of us looked eighteen. We've both grown a lot, though, and Marshall's even got a mustache. Hell, Alvin Collins just turned seventeen.

Perhaps it's cruel to think about leaving Susanne alone with Uncle Silas and Aunt Darcy. But sometimes I feel like my muscles are ready to jump out of my skin for wanting to do something besides tend this farm. So why shouldn't I go?

Poor Susanne. Though we quarrel sometimes, she understands me better than anyone. She ought to, being my twin. I'd hate to leave her behind. Still, she's hardheaded, not quick to cry, and almost as strong as I am. The scars on her arms have not rendered them useless, only disfigured. I bet that if I were to enlist, she'd be able to run this place almost as good as I do.

I can't go on like this with life passing me by. What kind of man will I be ten years from now if I can't look back and say "that was my *decision, I made it, and that's what I did"?*

A boy has to become a man. And it's high time everyone knows I'm not just a boy anymore.

3

"GRACIOUS, AND JUST what has become of your hat?" asked Aunt Darcy, her wrinkled fists thrust upon her bony hips, her rheumy gray eyes staring at Susanne as the girl straightened the covers on the bed they shared in one of the three upstairs rooms. Susanne and Darcy were dressed except for their shoes, with Aunt Darcy in her old brown frock with the velvet buttons and Susanne in her plain blue dress with the round white collar and black velvet bow at the neck. It was early in the morning, just after five-thirty, and the sky outside the window was barely awake, shimmering in shades of blue and plum. Mockingbirds and larks could be heard in the trees near the farmhouse. On the chest by the bed a single candle burned, throwing light and shadows over the walls and floor. Downstairs, Uncle Silas was already in the midst of his morning coughing fit, with racks so loud it shook the floor beneath Susanne's feet. Across the hall in another bedroom, Stephen was thumping around, getting ready for the day.

"I believe it's in the barn," said Susanne. She did not look at her aunt, but continued fluffing the feather pillows and placing them at the bed's head. "I broke a tie, and removed it so it wouldn't fall into the trough while I was brushing Molly last evening."

"Mercy, child!" said the old woman. Her voice was as dry as a seed pod in autumn. She eased herself down on the chair by the window with a groan, and leaned over with great effort to put on her shoes. "A young lady should not be dilly-dallying with horses!" Aunt Darcy panted as drew up the laces. "Dilly-dallying, no! Caring for horses are a man's duty. Your mother would turn in her grave if she knew you were behaving in such a manner!"

Susanne bit her tongue so she would not reply that it was her mother who had taught her to ride a horse and her mother who had taught her to groom, tack, and care for a horse. Her mother had been a strong-willed and capable woman, able to cook, sew, nurse, and garden, as all women did, but she was also able to chop wood and mend fences and assist with the birthing of a foal. Aunt Darcy, however, was raised to be a "lady," and in spite of the fact that the farm on which they lived was now tumbling into various degrees of disrepair—for although the twins worked as best they could they had a difficult time keeping up with the entire place—the old woman held to the firm belief that a woman was the weaker sex and commanded of God to do only that which did not "bring up a glow nor harden the hands." It did no good to argue with the old woman, but Susanne had learned over the past four years that her great-aunt was more of a grumbler than a disciplinarian. She said what she thought but then forgot what she'd said, and Susanne and Stephen were most often free to handle things in their own manner.

And so she only said with a sigh, "I shall find my hat as soon as we are done with our breakfast."

"I should think so," said Aunt Darcy. She finished with the first shoe, then unlaced it and tied it up two more times. "We've not got the income we once had," she continued. "No, no, we do not. Now that there are sewing machines we certainly do not. We cannot be neglectful with what we have. We must be careful." The first shoe finished, she bent to the second. She would not be done with this shoe, either, until it had been laced and tied thrice.

"Yes, ma'am," said Susanne.

Aunt Darcy finished her second shoe and hoisted herself to her feet, teetering for a moment then catching her balance. Susanne draped the quilt over the blanket rack at the foot of the bed and then placed her nightdress into the tall oak highboy. She and her aunt then took turns peering into the small looking glass to see that they were presentable to the world downstairs. Although Darcy, in her fear of the woods, never ventured outside anymore, so what could it matter how she looked? Susanne wished they had a large mirror on the chest like she had had back in Rhode Island, but Aunt Darcy said it was bad luck to be able to see one's whole self at a time. When Susanne had asked why, the old woman had only shuddered and replied, "It's not for me to say."

As Susanne held the little tortoise-shell backed mirror up for her aunt, Aunt Darcy smoothed her white hair with a mother-of-pearl backed hairbrush and then pinned on her cap with shaking fingers. Then she took it off, put it back, and pinned it, then repeated the motion a third time. Every morning she did this. She could not go with only putting the cap on once. There were many such behaviors Aunt Darcy did over and over, day after day.

"There now," said Aunt Darcy, pinching her cheeks with her fingers in hopes to bring out a glow. It failed miserably. "That's done. Done. Done." She reached for her shawl on the bedpost.

Susanne propped the looking glass against a pillow and braided, coiled, and pinned up her own long hair as her aunt slowly made her way into the hall and down the rickety steps. When Susanne was done, she stepped back as far as she could to try to catch her whole reflection but it was impossible. *It doesn't matter what you look like,* she told herself sternly. *You are plain and scarred, and that's the simple truth. It is probably best that there is no full mirror here, or you'd waste time looking for something that just isn't there.* She took a deep breath then picked up the mirror from the pillow and turned it face down on the chest. It didn't matter that she was not beautiful like her friend Marjorie. She was smart and she was patient. She would not need to attract a husband of wealth, because she and Stephen would someday inherit this farm and never want for shelter.

She plopped onto the chair to put on her own shoes.

"Good morning!" came a voice from the doorway. It was Stephen, his fingers holding the sill, his face peering in.

"Good morning," Susanne said. "You look dreadful. Your hair's straight up like a soldier saluting an officer."

"Yes sir, General Susanne," Stephen said with a touch of humored grumbling as he raked his fingers through his light brown hair and rolled his green eyes. He had the same coloring as his sister, and though he was a head taller, it was easy at first glance to know they were brother and sister, and not a surprise to find that they were twins. Stephen was dressed in gray trousers and a white shirt. His suspenders, buttoned to the waistband of his trousers, dangled to his knees. He shrugged them up and snapped them over his shoulders. "All done, sir! Anything else, sir?"

"Well," said Susanne, grinning in return, getting up and joining him in the hall. "I say you shall cook my breakfast and curry my horse and feed the chickens and hoe the beans for me today, as I shall be resting on the porch, soldier."

Stephen walked to the head of the steps, and glanced back. "Then, sir," he said with a salute, "consider this soldier a deserter, for I shall be nowhere near those chores you list!" With a laugh, he bounded downstairs.

Susanne followed her brother down to the front hall.

Uncle Silas was in his parlor bed by the fireplace, turned on his side and glaring at the two as they came in to greet him for the day. The old man's lips were curled over the few remaining teeth in his head. His eyebrows were as thick and gray as storm clouds. His breathing was raspy with the asthma.

"Good morning, Uncle Silas," said Stephen and Susanne nearly in unison as they passed his bed and headed for the door that led to the kitchen at the back of the house. Susanne picked up the bedpan from the floor by the bed, preferring not to look inside at the contents.

"Is it?" wheezed the old man. "I've not seen a good morning since I've been here in this bed! What I wouldn't give to be up and about like you young people, yet you don't appreciate how healthy you are!"

Susanne grit her teeth and went into the kitchen behind her brother. It did no good to argue with her uncle.

Aunt Darcy was at the chunky wooden table in the center of the room, potatoes all in a spin where she'd dropped them, a large chopping knife in her hand. The egg-collecting bucket was on the corner of the table.

The kitchen was a spacious room, and shared its stone fireplace with the parlor. There were openings in both sides of the wall, allowing the family to warm themselves in the hearth of one room and cook in the other. A large cast-iron cookstove sat on the kitchen floor in front of the fireplace, with a black pipe vented up through the flue in the wall. This stove had belonged to Susanne and Stephen's parents, and was one of the few things that had come by wagon with the twins four years earlier. Until then, Aunt Darcy had cooked directly in the fireplace like her mother and grandmother before her.

But the stove was not often used for cooking in the late spring and summer. From April until September, unless it was raining, Susanne baked and boiled in the large Dutch oven in the backyard. She and her aunt prepared the food inside then Susanne hauled it out to the yard.

All around the kitchen were Aunt Darcy's culinary tools—pots and pans sat on shelves that reached all the way to the ceiling. There was an apple peeler and a juicer, a set of knives and whisks, and a large spoon. From the rafters hung braids of dried apples, peppers, and mint and sage from the garden. A churn stood in the corner by the back door.

"Get that oven going," Aunt Darcy said to Stephen as he opened the door to the back stoop. A fly buzzed in on a cool spring breeze. "Silas won't care to wait for breakfast. No, he doesn't like to wait. Not at all. No."

"No, ma'am," said Stephen, not even trying to hide the irritation in his voice. He snatched the ax from beside the door and went out into the early morning sun. Susanne put the egg bucket over her elbow and followed with the bedpan.

"Does she need to tell me every morning what to do?" complained Stephen as he pulled the back door closed behind him and paused on the dirt pathway that cut from the stoop through the backyard and to the far fence by the barn. Chickens ran up to them and around their feet, seeking feed. "Every morning she repeats herself," he continued, "as if I haven't a brain in my head! Father and Mother never treated us such." He slammed the ax head down on the ground, sending up a puff of dust from the path.

"Mother and Father really cared for us," said Susanne with a tightening of her jaw. "Mother and Father loved us."

"How they were related to those old people is a mystery to me," continued Stephen, "for they are nothing but a vexation to the spirit!"

"Shhhh," said Susanne. "The kitchen window is part open."

Stephen shrugged. "Oh? Will anything I say make any difference to them? They only know we exist because we chop the wood and empty the urine!"

"Try not to let them vex you," said Susanne. "Aunt Darcy is annoying but harmless, and Uncle Silas is loud but can barely move. It does no good to let it get under your skin."

"Pah!" Stephen swore, then went around the side of the house to the woodshed to gather and chop wood to start the fire in the Dutch oven.

Susanne took the side path off the main one to the privy. She opened the creaking door, knocked aside spiders' webs that had accumulated overnight, and tossed the contents of the bedpan down the hole in the privy seat. Then she came back out and latched the door shut. Gnats and flies hummed around her face and she brushed them off. From the field across the creek, several cows mooed, the sound low and persistent. From the barn on the other side of the back fence, Fury and Molly nickered, knowing grain and water would soon be on its way.

Darcy and Silas Preston's farm, "Sycamore Grove," had at one time been a profitable cattle business, breeding Kerry cows for market as well as raising corn for profit. It consisted of nearly 120 acres three miles to the north of Gettysburg off the Harrisburg Road, touching the boundary of the Smith farm to the west and Pratt's Woods to the north, with the winding Rock Creek cutting through its center. It had been built in 1790 by Darcy's parents, Josiah and Mary Morton Barnes. Darcy had been born in 1792, one of six children. Only she and her sister Isabelle survived to adulthood. The other four had perished before their eighteenth birthdays; three of consumption and one from a cow-kick to the head. Isabelle married and moved to Philadelphia. Darcy married and remained on the farm with her husband, Silas Preston, a merchant who had come north from South Carolina. Isabelle and her husband Quentin had three children, one of which was Stephen and Susanne's father, Lucas. At age nineteen, Lucas attended the Lutheran Theological Seminary in Gettysburg and then, once ordained, moved to Rhode Island. He married Ella Susanne Ficks and there, Susanne and Stephen were born.

Under the care of Darcy and Silas Preston, the farm had continued to thrive with cattle and crops. The couple raised two daughters, Beatrice and Rudine. Beatrice died at fifteen from a broken and infected leg; Rudine married and moved to New Jersey. In spite of his Southern sympathies, Silas Preston made a few friends among the farmers in Adams County. Darcy served as pianist for the Methodist Church on the other side of Harrisburg Road from the farm, and occasionally hosted picnics and socials for the neighbors. She even let itinerant preachers set up camp meetings in the field in the spring before the land was tilled for planting.

But, as Susanne and Stephen had learned soon after their arrival, at some point Darcy had become touched in the head, and Uncle Silas had grown ill. The farm was no longer kept in good repair. Most of the cattle was sold for cash money, as were a number of the valuable items that had belonged to the family. Susanne's friend, Marjorie Olson, whose family lived on the next farm, had told Susanne what she could remember. Silas Preston lost his farmer friends when he no longer had the money to keep them entertained with cards and gambling in town. Why, Marjorie said honestly, would Northern men care to spend time with a loyal Southern man if he was no longer rich? They had nothing in common, and could no longer ignore each others' differences over stout ale and fine beers. And not long afterwards, Darcy had become peculiar—refusing to go outside except for her yard and then later, refusing to go outside the house. The old woman would repeat behaviors to distraction, babbling about a ghost in the woods. Marjorie had no idea what had set the old woman off, but knew it had happened and was sorry for Susanne that it had. "She was a lovely woman," Marjorie had told Susanne. "A shame you did not know her before she, well, before."

Very rarely did neighbors visit Sycamore Grove, and when Susanne and Stephen were in town, it was hard to answer the curious question of "How fare your aunt and uncle?" Susanne would mumble, "Fine, thank you," knowing it was a lie but not wanting to share embarrassing details. Stephen would ignore the question all together.

Susanne went into the hen house beside the privy. It was dark and dust flew like insects. "Good morning, ladies," she said to the birds. "Sorry, but I need your eggs. You wouldn't want Great Uncle Silas chastising me for no breakfast, would you?" Hens fluttered from their straw beds as Susanne gathered eight eggs and put them into the bucket. She then trudged back to the house to the tune of Stephen's chopping, and closed the kitchen door behind her.

"I heard mice in the cellar again, all night long!" called Uncle Silas. "I thought we bought new traps in town. What in the Lord's good earth are they being used for if not those blasted mice in the cellar?"

Susanne handed the egg-bucket to her aunt, then took the bedpan to the parlor. Uncle Silas' face was aglow; he always seemed to enjoy a row. It was as if it were the only thing that made him feel alive. He was on his side in the bed, his eyes lit up.

"I set the traps down there," said Susanne.

"You mustn't have put any bait inside."

Susanne slid the pan below the side of the bed. "I put bait inside," she said.

Uncle Silas' nose twitched beneath the stubble of his not-yet-shaved face, then he said, "Check them."

"I . . ." began Susanne, but then Aunt Darcy called from the kitchen. "Gracious, I can't prepare breakfast by myself!"

Susanne took a deep breath. "I shall check them after breakfast, Uncle Silas."

The morning ran its usual course. Once Stephen had the fire going in the Dutch oven and was off to give grain and water to the horses and the mule, Susanne and Aunt Darcy fixed a potato pie and boiled eggs, and then cut slices of cold ham for breakfast. It was ready by seven-thirty, and the family gathered at the large table in the parlor to eat. Uncle Silas, who Stephen had helped to his chair, mumbled thanks to God for meat and drink. Aunt Darcy added, "And bless our brave men at war. Do not let them come to harm. May they bring our poor country back together, as You will."

"Amen," said Stephen and Susanne together.

"Hmph," grumbled Uncle Silas.

The meal was eaten in silence, except for Uncle Silas' loud breathing and his occasional comments about the potatoes being tough and the milk being sour. Afterwards, Darcy and Susanne cleaned the dishes, and Stephen went outside to add new boards to the rotting barn loft. Susanne checked the mouse traps in the cellar. There were five traps, laid in the corners of the dirt-floor room, and in each trap was a dead little mouse. Susanne took them out, and holding them by the tails, went up the steps to the parlor and presented them ceremoniously to her uncle.

"The traps are working," she said.

"Not well enough. I can hear those mice all night long," complained Uncle Silas, then he flopped himself over in bed to face the wall, and said nothing more.

By noontime, Susanne was done with her chores in the house and able to go work outside, her favorite place in all the world. For it was there she felt free and happy. She ran down to the barn holding her skirt, tipping her head back to catch the warmth of the spring sunshine. Everything smelled wonderful outdoors—new grass, the lush blooms of the purple lilac, the damp mud along the banks of Rock Creek, the freshly-tilled soil in the garden and corn field, ready for planting. Back in Rhode Island she spent a great deal of time outdoors with her mother, a lover of nature, and even now, the caress of the sun on her face was like the touch of her mother's hand.

Passing through the gate that lead to the barnyard, Susanne called, "Stephen? You promised to help me with fertilizing those corn acres! I shall not and will not be hauling manure and those heavy bags of superphosphate on my own. What are you doing?"

From inside the barn, Stephen called, "The loft is repaired, but now I'm on the latch your Molly decided to chew from her stall door! She nearly had it off, and would have been in the grain room if I hadn't caught it in time!"

Susanne stepped over several foraging chickens at her feet and stopped at the open doorway to the barn. *That horse!* she thought with a smile. *Always making nuisance, just like she did back in Rhode Island!*

"It's mostly done," said Stephen from the shadows within the barn. "And I've got the superphosphate and manure loaded in the wagon. Groom Tim and get the harness ready. I'll be with you in a moment."

The mule and horses were in the paddock on the other side of the barn, put out so their stalls could be cleaned later. They stood side by side, nose to rear to nose, swishing flies from each other's faces with their respective tails. Tim, the mule, was a full hand taller than the horses, with ears that didn't seem to know which direction was forward or back. They flopped to and fro like cattails in the wind.

"Don't get too comfortable," Susanne said as she pushed up her sleeves, opened the paddock gate, and took hold of the mule's halter. "You've got work to do today."

Tim sniffed at Susanne's arm as if he thought she had brought a treat. She scratched his muzzle and led him outside to the wagon. He stood patiently as she pulled a few stray hitchhiking briars from his mane and tail.

Suddenly, Molly and Fury let out loud, rumbling whinnies, and began trotting around the paddock with ears pricked and nostrils flared.

"What's wrong?" Susanne said. "Is a storm coming? We need rain. This dust is dreadful."

Both horses slid to a stop by the paddock fence, and stared out at the lane which lead between the fields and out to Harrisburg Road. They snorted loudly. Susanne put her hand on Tim's side and looked out over his back to see what had caught the horses' attention. Then she saw it; several horses and a wagon moving up the lane toward the house. Dust rose behind them like smoke.

"Who is that coming here?" Susanne asked aloud. "I don't know those horses."

She squinted, but couldn't make out anything clearly except two dark horses, a smaller light one, and the wagon.

"Stephen!" she called. "Are we expecting company today?"

"No," Stephen answered from the barn.

Susanne watched the approaching entourage. "Folks are coming. I don't know who. Several horses, it seems."

Stephen appeared at the window of Molly's stall. His face was tight. "It could be Confederates!"

Susanne caught her face in her hands. "What did you say?"

"Maybe it's the Confederates!"

"Oh, dear God, I hope not!" Susanne looked back over Tim's back, clutching his stubby mane between her fingers. The horses and wagon on the lane were nearer now, though she still could not make out the features of the travelers. Rumors had been bantered about in town over the past month that the Confederate Army had sent divisions into Pennsylvania, and that they burned farms and stole horses. No one in Gettysburg had seen the dreaded Rebels, but the stories abounded, and the citizens of town had actually sent many of their valuables to family members in Philadelphia and Baltimore just in case the invasion ever came. Men would stand outside stores and at the train station, arms crossed, swearing in their loudest voices that they were prepared, that they had arms at home ready to do the talking to any filthy Reb who mistakenly wandered too close.

Susanne spun away from Tim and called to Stephen. "We have to lock the house and hide upstairs!" She raced around the barn, slammed open the gate, and headed up the path toward the house. Chickens in the yard scattered like milkweed fluff in the wind, squawking loudly. It was only a moment before Stephen was by Susanne's side, taking the ground in stride with his longer legs.

"Aunt Darcy!" he shouted as he reached the back door ahead of Susanne. He slammed open the door and fell into the kitchen. Susanne was a few steps behind him.

Aunt Darcy was in the kitchen, sweeping with her birch broom. It fell with a clatter to the pinewood floor.

"Aunt Darcy, I think it's Rebels coming!" said Stephen.

"Rebels?" she wailed. "God have mercy on our souls!"

Susanne took her aunt by the arm and steered the woman through the door into the parlor. "We have to get upstairs," Susanne said. "Stephen, load the rifle and take it to the front stoop to scare them off! Hurry!"

On his bed, Uncle Silas had pushed himself up on his elbow. "Confederates? Get me up outa this bed! Let me talk to them. They won't steal from a fellow Southerner!"

"You must stay put, Uncle Silas!" said Stephen.

As Stephen snatched the rifle from the rack over the fireplace and grabbed a packet of shot and powder from the small writing desk, Susanne tugged and pulled her aunt to the stairs. The old woman froze there, looking back over her shoulder at the tall windows to either side of the front door. Through the glass, the unknown visitors could be seen pulling their wagon up to the front gate. Susanne's throat tightened; the blood in the backs of her hands flushed cold.

"Aunt Darcy, please!" she urged. Her aunt's arm was fragile, she knew, but she tugged anyway. A bruise would be better than a kidnapping.

"Get me up, I say!" demanded Uncle Silas. He was struggling with his bedcover, battling them as if they were an enemy unto themselves. "Stephen, get me up!"

Stephen had the rifle between his knees, and was dumping the shot and powder into the barrel. There was a line of sweat on his lip. He glanced up at Susanne as she prodded her aunt up the steps in front of her. Susanne read the fear in his face, and it made her own heart beat even faster.

Susanne and Aunt Darcy reached the top of the steps, with the old woman panting and trembling. Susanne heard the front door yank open and Stephen's booted feet scramble out to the stoop. Susanne ran up the hall to the front window, to peer outside and see what danger was indeed facing. Aunt Darcy stood twisting the hem of her apron in her hand and saying, "Oh, oh, sweet Jesus, oh!"

The wagon could be seen clearly from the second floor vantage point. There were three horses; a swaybacked sorrel, black in the harness, and a small gray pony tied to the rear. In the wagon bed was a huge stack of crates and bundles. A man in dark clothing and a dust-laden top hat was unlatching the gate and swinging it wide to allow a young boy in a large hat and a woman in the fullest green skirt Susanne had ever seen pass through. The boy had his fists clenched and his shoulders hunched. The woman held her chin up haughtily beneath the broad brim of her flowered bonnet.

A woman and a child? These were the dreaded Rebels come to strip the farm bare of it's livestock and food?

"Ho!" called Stephen from the stoop below. "Who are you?"

The man pushed back his hat, revealing a face equally coated in dust. "Son! Lower that weapon!" he said. "No need to be rude to family!"

Family? Susanne thought.

"Family?" Stephen asked.

The woman caught up with the man and pressed her gloved hand to her chest as if offended. The boy stood behind her, kicking at a loose stone on the walkway. He seemed to be very pale; the backs of his hands at the ends of his jacket sleeves looked as white as river pebbles. "Why certainly, family," the woman said in a nasal voice. "Did Mother not tell you that Simon and I were coming today?"

No, thought Susanne.

"No," said Stephen, stepping off the stoop and into Susanne's view. The rifle was pointed toward the ground now. "Your mother is Aunt Darcy? You are Rudine?"

The woman frowned beneath the brim of her hat. "That is Aunt Rudine to you. I won't tolerate such familiarity."

So this is Rudine, thought Susanne. *She seems to be as unpleasant as her father!*

"Susanne," said Aunt Darcy from the top of the stairs. Her voice was trembling. "Who is it? Who is here?"

"It's not rebels," said Susanne without looking back. "It's Rudine. I mean Aunt Rudine. And a boy and a man."

"Oh!" gasped Aunt Darcy, and she shuffled to the window beside Susanne. "Rudine! She wrote and said she was coming! I forgot she was coming!"

Susanne sighed deeply, hoping her frustration didn't show. But beneath the frustration was a new fear; the wagon by the gate was loaded, obviously filled with personal items. Obviously Rudine and her son had come planning to stay for a long time. Susanne had grown used to having the run of the farm with Stephen. Granted, Rudine and Simon weren't Confederates ready to burn and pillage, but this couldn't be good, either.

Susanne followed her aunt downstairs to the front hall, where Stephen was holding the door for the three visitors. Rudine came through first, her skirt squeezing through the door frame, followed by the dusty man and the pale boy. Stephen gave Susanne a strained look; she knew he was feeling the same anxiety as she.

"Rudine, darling!" exclaimed Aunt Darcy, lifting her arms carefully and taking her daughter in a delicate embrace. Rudine stood straight as her mother hugged her, as if hugging were improper. Her eyes turned toward Susanne and the expression was one of cool analysis.

"And this is Susanne?" she asked, pulling away from her mother and tilting her head critically.

"Yes," said Susanne. "Ma'am." She curtsied.

"Oh," said Rudine, glancing Susanne up and down and pausing at the scarred arms. Susanne quickly tugged her sleeves down to her wrists. "I see." Rudine's voice said it all. She was not at all impressed with her niece.

"Rudine!" called Uncle Silas from the parlor. "Daughter, come in! Let me see you! It's been such a long time!"

"Yes, Father, it is I," said Rudine. She lifted a gloved hand toward the boy and said, "This is my son Simon. He is thirteen. And this is Mr. Robert Issel, from Trenton. He was kind enough to accompany Simon and myself here with his wagon and horses. A good 3 days he's been away from his family on our behalf."

Aunt Darcy nodded as Mr. Issel bowed slightly. "Thank you kindly, sir. Surely a lady should not travel alone with her son. But what of your wagon, Rudine? Your horses?"

Simon, who stood cowering by the door, spoke at

last, his voice shrill and thin. "Sold them," he said. "Had to. House, too. S'all gone." His lower lip went out in a pout.

Susanne looked at Stephen; Stephen looked at Susanne. Rudine and Silas had not come to visit. They'd come to stay.

"Rudine?" called Silas from the parlor.

"Did you not receive my letter, Mother?" insisted Rudine.

"Oh," said Aunt Darcy. "I did. But I forgot, dear me. My poor girl! Everything gone, and your husband run off !"

Rudine untied the strings to her bonnet and lifted it from her primly braided hair, and said, "Run off, Mother. You have a way of making things sound quite crude. He left to join the army. He left to do his duty for the Union."

"He left nearly a year ago," said the pale boy, removing his hat as well. He looked up at Susanne. She was surprised to see that his eyes were without color, and seemingly ringed in pink. "He hasn't written us since he left. If he was dead, the captain would have sent word. I think—"

Rudine spun about and drove her open hand across the boy's face. His white skin blushed red where her hand struck. "Hush! Not a word on what you think!" She took her son by the arm as the boy let out a ear-piercing whine, and over the noise said to her mother, "We are fine, Simon and I. Perhaps we sold a few things to pay for a few minor debts, but we were never better! No one is to find pity for us, I assure you." She then directed her son into the parlor to see Uncle Silas. Aunt Darcy followed meekly.

Mr. Issel looked at Susanne and shrugged. Then he said in a near-whisper, "That's quite some lady. She has . . . opinions, and no one best argue with her."

"Oh," said Susanne. "I see."

"I think you best see," said Mr. Issel with a shake of

his head, "if you want to have peace with this woman. Three days on the road and I could swear it was three weeks."

Susanne, Stephen, and Mr. Issel went into the parlor. Rudine stood beside her father's bed, her hands folded, her mouth set in a serious line. "So ill, I see!" she was saying. "I shall do all I can to help you recover from your ailments. Has no one called a doctor? Has no one found medicines to help you? Do they do nothing for you, poor man?" Rudine glanced at Susanne and Great-aunt Darcy, her eyes flashing with blame.

"I should go now," said Mr. Issel, rolling his top hat in his hands. "Good day to you all."

"But Mr. Issel," said Susanne. "Such a long journey and you need a meal. We are to have our supper in but an hour or so. You must stay. We've venison and tea."

"Ah, thank you, no," said the man, his voice barely disguising the relief at his imminent departure. "But I've friends in Gettysburg with whom I plan to visit today. I thank you, but will be leaving."

Farewells and thanks were made, and then Mr. Issel was gone in his wagon, down the lane at a rapid clip. Aunt Rudine sent Stephen outside to collect the trunks and crates Mr. Issel had left in front of the house. These were taken upstairs to the bedroom Susanne and Darcy shared. Simon's smaller cases were put into Stephen's bedroom.

"Now," said Aunt Rudine, turning about in the middle of the room, appraising her new situation, as Susanne, Aunt Darcy, Simon and Stephen looked on. "Stephen, show Simon where to stable his pony. Don't let it be some damp corner, either. That pony cost a pretty penny."

Stephen said, "Come on," to the thin, pale Simon, and the two went downstairs. "Are their rats in your barn?" Susanne could hear Simon say in his wavering, high-pitched voice. "I don't like rats! Rats are nasty! You ever been bitten by a rat? It could make you go insane and die!" The front door slammed after them.

Aunt Rudine turned to Susanne. "And now, young lady, you will move your things to the front room, as I will be sharing with my mother."

Susanne knew her face showed her shock, but she didn't care. Was she to have to obey this woman she didn't even know, someone who came barging in to her life and began making changes? "Excuse me? There is no bed. It is where Aunt Darcy sews. There is a table and chair and sewing notions, nothing else!"

But it was clear Aunt Rudine was not used to being challenged. She pointed a stern finger at Susanne. "Remember yourself, Susanne. Children are to be seen and not heard. Gather your clothes and whatever items are about this room, and take them out. We shall find a suitable mattress for you, or shall make one. You can sew a tick, can you not? But I shall never hear you speak in such a manner to me again. Do you understand?"

"Children?" Susanne said, her neck flushing hot with fury. "I . . . I am not a child!"

"You behave as one," said Rudine. "And I can see you've gotten away with that here. Pity! Well, we shall correct that, shall we not, Mother?"

Susanne looked at Aunt Darcy, who was frowning and dabbing her face with her handkerchief. Surely the older woman would support her and not let this newcomer take control. But Aunt Darcy appeared cowed by her daughter's assertiveness, and said nothing.

Without another word, Susanne went to the highboy, tugged open the doors, and began removing her dresses. And as she hauled the first armload of petticoats and stockings to her new room, she thought, *Correct this, indeed! Oh, we shall correct this, and it shan't be me who is changed! It will be the bossy Aunt Rudine. She will not be the boss here! She will not!*

4

HARRISBURG ROAD LEADING south into Gettysburg was worn and pitted, and the pitching of the wagon seat jarred Stephen's teeth. His friend Marshall Fenwick, a tall boy of fifteen with curly yellow hair, an equally curly mustache and a ruddy face, had caught up with Stephen on the road, and now sat next to him, chewing on a piece of cheese he'd had in his pocket.

Susanne had wanted to come into town this morning, but Aunt Rudine had forbidden it. But Simon was along for the journey, straggling far behind on his small white pony. The boy gripped the reins of his mount nervously, as if he was afraid Stephen and Marshall might break the mule into a gallop and leave him behind, which, to Stephen, would have been a dandy thing to do to be rid of the whining boy. Aunt Rudine and Simon had been living at Sycamore Grove two weeks. It felt like an eternity. Rudine was ruling the roost and trying to make Susanne behave properly. Simon was always underfoot and complaining. Stephen could hardly believe it, but he had begun wishing for the days when it was just Uncle Silas griping.

"Wait for me!" Simon called, digging his heels into the sides of his pony, who refused to be coaxed. "Sally can't keep up with you."

"Sally can keep up just fine," Marshall called back. "She's just smart enough to know where you belong."

"Aw," Simon moaned, a sudden wind tugging at his hat and tussling his stark white hair.

Stephen and Marshall looked at each other and chuckled. But then Stephen said with a sigh, "I had to bring him. Uncle Silas insisted. He thinks the sun will do something for Simon's complexion and attitude."

"You sure it won't wilt him like a daisy?"

Stephen shrugged. "I sometimes wonder if all those times Aunt Darcy has seen that ghost of hers it wasn't just Simon out playing in the woods. Whoooo! Whooooooooo!"

They laughed, and Simon, just out of earshot, called, "What's so funny?" But Stephen ignored him. It was the best solution to a vexing situation.

Two crates of cabbages and several deer hides lay in the back of the wagon. Stephen was to get rid of the cabbages for either cash or trade, and take the hides to the tannery for cash. Sometimes he had the hides cured for Aunt Darcy so she could stitch them into jackets, belts, and haversacks. For many years, Darcy Preston had sewn fine dresses, shirts, and coats for neighbors and had brought in a reasonable profit from it. But other seamstresses in town, such as Mrs. Schriver and Jennie Wade and her mother, had several years earlier purchased Singer sewing machines and were able to do the work in less than half the time. Now, however, cotton cloth was very hard to come by. The South produced the fiber, and they weren't about to share their wealth with their enemies in the north. Yet the Schrivers and the Wades were able to find other materials such as wool and linen to run through their sewing machines. Some ladies even took old cotton dresses to the seamstresses to have them transformed into garments for their children, or napkins, or hand towels. But Aunt Darcy sewed only for her family these days. And the need for money outweighed the need for new clothes.

As the three boys drew closer to Gettysburg, they came upon more horses and wagons, some carrying baskets of food and clothing that Stephen guessed was to be delivered to the Union Army. Most of the local people—unlike Uncle Silas—faithfully supported the war effort, and gladly offered what materials they could spare to assist the army, which constantly needed supplies.

Minutes later they entered the town limits, over the railroad tracks by the station, through the town square known by its nickname the "Diamond," and steered southward toward the center of town on Baltimore Street. Here, Stephen felt a thrill of excitement he could never know at the farm. The sounds and smells of the community made him long yet again for something different, something new. Something daring.

Gettysburg was not a large city, but it lay at a major crossroads so that there was always plenty of commerce and activity within its borders. Stephen drove the wagon past a bank, the Courthouse, the office of the weekly Gettysburg *Courier,* several taverns, houses, gardens, a carriage maker, and a large general store with a broad verandah where elderly gentlemen sat in the shade engaged in a lively conversation. Men and women strolled the brick sidewalks and crossed the dirt streets to tend to business, while carriages, wagons, and carts rattled to and fro. There were a few blacks in town—maids, blacksmith assistants, clerks. No slaves, of course, for this was the North. This was a free state. Stephen had never even seen a slave, though slavery was one of the reasons the country was now torn apart by a vicious Civil War.

To the west between the two- and three-story brick and weatherboard buildings, Stephen could catch glimpses of Seminary Ridge. On that hill the Lutheran Theological

School stood. Stephen's father Lucas Daniel Blackburn had studied there to become a Lutheran minister. Directly south down Baltimore Street, Cemetery Hill rose like the back of a very large and tired old dog.

As the wagon reached the intersection of High Street, there came around the corner a handful of blue-coated figures, some of them seemingly no older than Stephen. Most carried muskets, and one of them, an officer, had a sabre at his side. All of them had proud, beaming faces, but they walked quietly and with dignity. Stephen pulled the mule up to watch them pass, and pushed back the brim of his hat to have a better look. Stephen and Marshall raised their hands in greeting, and some of the young soldiers smiled, but none waved back. Across the street, a few young women in summer frocks had gathered and were pointing at the soldiers. One was Jennie Wade, a girl a few years older than Stephen but one, nonetheless, who he found rather pretty.

"Look at those soldiers," Stephen said to Marshall. "Such respect they get."

"From the women," said Marshall. "I see Jennie smiling at them." He winked at Stephen. He knew Stephen had taken a fancy, but also knew Stephen was too shy to speak to her.

"Well, certainly," said Stephen. "The women. And the men. And the children. Everyone honors our soldiers. What I wouldn't do to trade places."

"Indeed," said Marshall. "We'll never get any respect in Gettysburg. Especially not with the little ghost following us." He nodded at Simon, who trailed them a half-block. "If only we'd been old enough to enlist with Gettysburg's Second Pennsylvania Volunteers in April two years ago. We have had this war done with, they'd had us! Yes, sir!"

"If only," said Stephen.

Stephen worked the mule and wagon right onto Breckenridge. Ahead two blocks was the tannery owned by George Bowler. Mr. Bowler was a pleasant man who had attended Seminary with Lucas Blackburn before deciding he was better with animal hides than with God. Mr. Bowler's son Ethan, who was a few years older than Stephen, had gone off to war almost a year before. Stephen was anxious to know how Ethan was faring and if, unlike the often dreary reports in the *Daily Gazette,* the Union was finally beating the tar out of the Rebels. The fighting in Virginia—and elsewhere in the South—had reportedly been fierce recently.

Marshall tied the mule to the post outside the tannery while Stephen paused to pick a stone from one of the mule's hooves. On the air was the thick, oily scent of leather and the sweet aroma of wood smoke. The two stepped up to the verandah of the big wooden building just as Simon came onto Breckenridge, his eyes wide and wary and his legs flapping against his pony in a futile effort to get her moving past a plodding trot. "Stephen!" he called out. "Hold up a moment, won't you?"

Stephen and Marshall went inside, where they found themselves facing a tall wooden counter and a door that led to the rear of the building. Removing his hat, Stephen rang the bell on the counter. A few moments later, the door to the back opened, and a stocky, middle-aged man with a vast beard, graying hair, and noticeable limp came through, wiping his hands on a dirty-looking apron.

"Hello, young gentlemen," came the man's booming voice. "And how are you this morning?"

"Fine, sir," said Stephen.

"Fine, Mr. Bowler," said Marshall.

"Marshall, your parents?"

"In excellent health."

"And Stephen, your aunt and uncle? How do they fare?"

Stephen coughed into his hand, and Marshall covered for him by pointing out the window. "We've nice hides for you today. Four of them!"

Mr. Bowler looked from Stephen to the window. "Yes, good. You and Stephen are two of the most skilled hunters in Adams County. 'Tis a shame you aren't old enough to join the army. I hear there's a regiment called Berdan's Sharpshooters. Best shots in all of the Union! They must be able to hit a ten inch target ten times from a distance of one hundred yards. I dare say you and Marshall could do as well. They dress in green uniforms and have special-issue rifles."

Stephen put one fist inside the other. Talk like that just made things worse. He could imagine himself easily shooting those targets and being given a green uniform. Uncle Silas would have no option but to see him as he was, not as the little boy he chose to imagine him as.

"These hides," said Mr. Bowler. "Selling or tanning?"

"Selling."

"Two dollars a hide." Mr. Bowler rang the bell on the counter, and a towheaded lad of about twelve came through the door, his face and hands filmed with brownish residue. "Henry, fetch the hides from these gentlemen's wagon, if you please." The boy nodded, gave Stephen and Marshall a shy smile, and hurried out the front door to his task.

"Who is that boy, Mr. Bowler?" asked Stephen.

The big man ran his fingers through his beard. "My nephew, Henry Harrington. From Cashtown. He's about the only help I can keep in here, bein' so many of our men have gone off with the Federals, God bless 'em. Ben Russell—you remember Ben, I'm sure—he enlisted in the army just last week. And of course, my own boy Ethan . . ." Mr. Bowler suddenly fell silent, his eyes taking on a far away gleam. Stephen and Marshall glanced at each other in bewilderment.

"How's Ethan?" Stephen asked carefully. "Is he fighting in Virginia?"

"Of course, you haven't heard about Ethan for you've not been in town for two weeks," Mr. Bowler said slowly. "He's come home just four days ago. Home for good."

"His enlistment is up already?" said Marshall incredulously. "Did he kill a bunch of rebels?"

"Son," said Mr. Bowler, his words slow, his jaw tight. "Ethan lost both of his legs in the fighting. He's home with his mother now. He did his duty. Lord, he did his duty."

Stephen was dumb-struck. He hadn't known Ethan Bowler well, but he could not envision the muscular, athletic young man as an invalid. How would he get about? Would he ever marry or hold a job? Stephen was suddenly aware of his own legs, of the muscles, skin, and bones, and wondered what it would feel like to have them gone.

"I'm very sorry," Stephen managed. "I didn't know . . . I wouldn't have asked . . . I . . ."

Mr. Bowler rubbed his arms. "Fighting for a good cause," he said. "Put our country back together. It's a good cause. Sometimes these things happen. Young men who do their duty sometimes are wounded. Killed. I'm proud of my son, make no mistake about that. Legs or no."

"Yes, sir, of course you are," Stephen managed.

The bearded man shook his head and thumped his fist on the counter. "Enough of this, you've got hides for me." He glanced through the window at his nephew. Outside, young Henry Harrington had gathered up the bundled hides and was carrying them around to the back of the building. "And I have cash money for you. Eight dollars total." He handed Stephen money from a box beneath the counter.

"Thank you, sir," Stephen said. He started to turn to leave, but then he paused and said to Mr. Bowler. "Tell Ethan I'm sorry to hear about his injury. And tell him I'm proud of him, too."

"So am I," Marshall added.

"So you are what?" The voice was just outside the

tannery door. Simon stood there with his hands on his hips and his arms crossed. He was covered with grit from the Gettysburg road, and his dark trousers were covered with light hairs from his pony's sweaty hide.

"Never you mind," said Marshall. "This is men talk. Good day, Mr. Bowler." Marshall and Stephen brushed past Simon and out to the street.

The white-haired boy gazed after them with puzzled eyes, squinting as though the sun hurt him in spite of the shade from his hat. "Stephen, you look terrible," said Simon. He took up his pony's reins from the post. "What's wrong?"

"Nothing's wrong with him," Marshall said.

"Come on," Simon said as if enjoying Stephen's obvious discomfort. "Something's got your nerves pretty good."

Marshall turned to Stephen. "You know, I'm thirsty. There's a well down near the hotel. What do you say we go get us a drink?"

"That'd be good," Stephen said, seeing the mischievous light in Marshall's eyes returning.

Marshall stepped up to Simon and leaned down in his face. "You, little boy," he said, suddenly thumping Simon on the head with the heel of his palm, "are a pest." Then, suddenly, he took off running. Stephen sprinted after Marshall, the thrill of the sudden escape allowing him to forget for a moment the grim feeling he'd had after talking to Mr. Bowler.

"What?" Simon cried from behind. "I'll tell on you!" Stephen looked back to see Simon frantically looping his pony's reins back over the post and taking off after his cousin.

As soon as they rounded the corner of Washington Street, Stephen and Marshall ducked behind a row of long wooden crates stacked next to a soot-coated brick building with a sign reading, "The O'Conner Trade and Warehouse Company."

They watched until Simon appeared. The boy's eyes

darted from left to right; his fists were locked furiously on his hips. Stephen could barely suppress a snicker as Simon took off running in the opposite direction.

"Maybe we should follow him but not let him see us," Marshall offered. "We could spook him by throwing rocks. He doesn't know his way around town like we do!"

"Wait," Stephen said, turning his attention from his friend to one of the crates, the lid of which had not been fastened down. "Hey!" He slid the wooden cover aside and pointed to the contents. "Rifles!"

On the side of the crate was stenciled "U.S. Model .58 Caliber. Quantity: 10. Springfield, Massachusetts Armory." He whistled softly. How he would love taking these out to have a better look.

"Ho there!" came a gruff voice from nearby. Stephen and Marshall flinched, and glanced up to see a burly, black-bearded figure approaching from around the corner of the building. His eyes glowered. "You boys get away from those. You got no business playing around here."

Stephen stood up, his pride bruised at being addressed in such derisive terms. "We are certainly not playing, sir. We're old enough to join up!"

The man gave them a contemptuous stare, then laughed mirthlessly. "Then get on out of here, little man. I'm sure you've got a wife and kids to take care of."

Stephen felt a tug on his sleeve. "Guess we'd better do as he says," Marshall grumbled.

The two of them turned and sauntered away, trying to maintain a relaxed pace. Stephen could feel the man's burning stare until they were well beyond his line of sight. *He thinks of us as children!* Stephen thought furiously.

"Guess we'd better get home to our wives and kids, don't you think?" he said sarcastically to Marshall.

"Ah, hold your tongue," muttered Marshall.

As they reached the corner and turned back onto Breckenridge, Stephen saw a bulletin nailed to the side of Walter Riley's tobacco shop. Printed at the top, in huge block letters, were the words "WANTED FOR SERVICE!" He grabbed Marshall's elbow and steered him to the notice. He read the paper aloud.

"Young men of good standing to enlist in the Army of the United States, for the purposes of bringing together the Union following the unlawful secession of those States hereby known as the Confederate States of America. Applicants must be at least eighteen years of age. Enlistments will take place at the Gettysburg Courthouse May 1–3."

A young man came up to stand beside Marshall and Stephen. He appeared to be about twenty years old, with stringy black hair and a hawk-nose. He smelled like cow manure. "Thinking to enlist?" he asked. "How old are you?"

"Eighteen, going on nineteen," Stephen said, surprising himself with the ease of his own lie.

"Oh?" queried the fellow, narrowing his eyes. "You're going on nineteen months shy of sixteen, if you ask me."

Stephen's ears flushed beneath his hat. "That's not so!"

"You wanting to join the Army?"

"What if I am?" demanded Stephen.

The young man looked around rather shiftily. "You play a horn? Drums, maybe?"

"No," Stephen said. "What difference does that make?"

"Just tell them you play a bugle. They don't care how old you are to be a bugler. Just tell them that."

"But I don't play."

"And you've never thought to lie about your age, either? Heavens above, you are a child!" And with that, the lanky young man turned and stalked away.

"Fancy that," Marshall said with a little grin. "We join the army to make music."

"There you are!" came a shrill voice that set Stephen's teeth on edge. "You thought you would lose me!"

"Simon," Stephen said, turning about, "I'd happily forgotten you exist."

"What are you reading there?" asked the boy.

"A proclamation from President Lincoln," Stephen said. "It reads, 'all persons who have been duly and officially recognized as sniveling brats are hereby ordered to remain indoors under lock and key until further notice. Any violation of this proclamation will result in the offender being skinned alive and served to the U.S. Army for their daily rations.' "

"After being rolled in cornmeal and boiled in oil," Marshall added with a chuckle.

Simon's face contorted with anger. "All you do is make fun of me and try to get rid of me. I'm telling Uncle Silas! I'm telling Uncle Silas!"

" 'I'm telling Uncle Silas!' " repeated Marshall with a shake of his head. "What an infant we have here, Stephen!"

Suddenly Simon rushed forward with arms flailing, catching Marshall across the jaw with a fist and sending him stumbling backward. Stephen lunged out to restrain his young cousin, but the boy turned on him and struck him across the cheek, tearing welts along Stephen's face with the rough fingernails. More surprised and angered than hurt, Stephen tackled the boy, shoving him to the ground and holding him down with all his weight. With the edge of his fist, he thumped Simon solidly on the top of the head.

"Stop this!" squealed Simon from beneath Stephen's bulk. "You've got no call to get ugly here!"

Marshall, regaining his balance, let loose a laugh. "Too late! Ugly's found a home on Simon's face."

Simon kicked and struggled all the more, but he

could not pitch Stephen off. Stephen thumped his head again, hoping to get through the youngster's temper.

"Be still and I'll let you get up. Be still now."

"I'm telling!" Simon screamed again. "I'm telling Uncle Silas and my mother on you!"

At last, when if felt as though most of the fire had gone out of his cousin, Stephen rolled off of him, stood up and brushed off his trousers. One of his suspenders had snapped and hung down his back. "Curses!" he swore. This was just another thing with which to deal. As Simon started to get up, still wailing that he was going to tell Uncle Silas, Marshall stepped up and gave the boy a shove, sending him sprawling into the dirt.

"That's for the punch," Marshall said. "We were only fooling with you."

"It didn't sound like foolin'!" said Simon. "You're going to be in trouble, just you wait!"

Stephen and Marshall turned away and started back to their wagon at the tannery. Behind them, Simon pulled himself to his feet and spat dust onto the ground. "You're gonna be sorry for being mean to me one of these days," he muttered half-heartedly.

As they walked, Stephen tried to shut out his cousin's whining, but to no avail. What had he done to deserve this kind of torture? The boy knew all the right ways to get under his skin, and did so mercilessly. Stephen had tried over the past two weeks to get along with Simon, but the boy simply wouldn't let him. All Stephen knew was that whenever he had to spend time with the lad, his stomach hurt.

They reached the wagon and Marshall untied the mule's reins from the hitching post. Stephen clambered up into the seat, grabbed up the reins, and then glanced back at Simon who was digging divots in the road with his feet as he went to untie his pony. As the wagon was set to rolling again, Stephen said, "I think we should do it."

"Enlist in the army?"

"Yes. If ever there was a time to get away, it's now."

Marshall was silent for a moment. The wagon crossed Middle Street and headed down the slope of Baltimore toward the train tracks. On the left side of the street, ladies were peering in the window of the bakery. On the right side, children were rolling hoops along the brick walkway. Stephen pulled the mule up as one hoop got away from a little girl and rolled across the road in the path of the wagon.

"So, what do you think?" Stephen asked Marshall as the little girl raced after the hoop. "Ethan Bowler got hurt, and that's bad. But he didn't ride as good as us. He didn't shoot as good as us. We'll be fine! We'll do great!"

"I think we should do it, and now," said Marshall. "When else, Stephen? We've talked about this forever."

"Stephen!" called Simon from behind.

Stephen slapped the mule's back with the reins and the wagon jerked back into motion. "The enlistment men will be at the courthouse in the morning," he said. "We'd have to leave early, before anybody's up. The folks would never let me go if they knew."

"Four-thirty, then, at Pritchett's Corners?"

Stephen's heart pounded with excitement and fear at the momentous decision he was about to make. He knew that once he decided, there was no going back on it. But he couldn't keep living this way. This was no way to grow into a man. "Four-thirty," he said. "Let's do it."

Marshall's face suddenly looked older and more serious, with none of his characteristic mischievous vigor. "We'll set the Rebels straight, that's what we'll do."

"What are you talking about up there?" shouted Simon.

"Nothing," Stephen called back, turning to look at his cousin with eyes that now shone with both determination and apprehension. "Nothing for you to know about, anyway."

5

May 7, 1863

Such a dreadful day it's been. Did I say day? I should say weeks! If Aunt Darcy and Uncle Silas have been an aggravation to Stephen and me these past four years, what is there to say of the last two weeks with Aunt Rudine? She is a wagon full of aggravations, a barn full, a mountain! She insists that I wear snoods over my hair and gloves on my hands when outside regardless of the chore, and hooped petticoats beneath my skirts at all times. "Oh," she said when I told her with great relief that I would happily comply but had no hoops to wear, "come, child, and see what extras I have in my trunk." Why, I can hardly fit through the door in that hoop, let alone the gate to the barn. But then what can it matter? Rudine insists I not go to the barn, and certainly won't let me ride a-straddle as I've always done. She's lent me a sidesaddle from the vast supply of odds and ends she brought from New Jersey. I must be gentile and curtsey and take up ladylike pursuits in my free time.

Free time. I've never wanted it nor needed it and now she insists on it. Every day after our mid-day meal, I must take up some ghastly and tedious hobby under the guise of free time. Embroidery. The flute. I want to be outside, spreading manure for the corn and alfalfa. I want to be feeding Tim to the wagon and grooming Molly. But she will not have it, and I must do as she says. If I do not, I fear she will send me away. And if she did, what would I do? Become a teacher? There are more ladies after such jobs now that the war is claiming husbands and brothers that there would be no place for me in a schoolhouse. Go join Marjorie at the factory? What I have never admitted to anyone, not even my dear Stephen, is that though there is much I am able to do, my scarred right arm cannot bend as well as it once did, nor can I lift with it more than a pound or two. I fear I would be let go from the factory after just a day when they saw the truth, and I would be penniless, homeless.

Yet, now that Aunt Rudine is here, what chance have I that this farm will be mine when Uncle Silas and Aunt Darcy are gone? Curses! And curses yet again!

I would give both Aunt Rudine and her boy Simon an Irish hoist if I had the courage, and send them back to New Jersey, rubbing their fine behinds! Good-bye!

Stephen and his friend Marshall took Simon into town this morning to get money for the hides of the deer they hunted last weekend. I wanted to go along, but of course, Aunt Rudine had other plans. I cleaned and baked, of which I have no complaints, but then we sat down at the parlor table and she gave to me a set of watercolor paints and a sheet of rough paper. She showed me how to dip the brush into a bowl of water and rub it on the paper. I'll admit, the colors were lovely, but I was about to jump out of my skin for wanting to be away from her supervision and wanting to be away from Uncle Silas and his annoying, gurgling, nap-time snoring. Aunt Rudine, as ladylike as always, ignored the noise and proceeded to tell me how to paint a flower, with delicate strokes of the brush and not the bold strokes I was prone to use.

At supper this evening, Aunt Rudine began chatting about tomorrow's noon tea and bandage-rolling. She has invited the neighboring ladies to come to Sycamore Grove for this, assuring Aunt Darcy that such a civil activity is good for the hands and good for the spirit. All her friends back in New Jersey had done so for our good men in blue. Aunt Darcy dabbed the corners of her mouth nervously with her napkin at the suggestion.

Uncle Silas growled, "We've not had visitors here in years. We're much better off without a bunch of gabbing hens! Especially them that support the war against the Confederacy!"

Simon said nothing. Rudine tried to cajole her father, for as much as she criticizes her mother she dotes on her father, regardless of his views. I rolled my eyes at Stephen. I thought Stephen would jump into the conversation, for he is quite devoted to the idea of the Union and the brave men who are trying to bring her back together, but tonight he said nothing. He just sat stirring his spoon in his beans, his eyebrows drawn down in a serious scowl. Something is occupying his mind. Tomorrow, I'll ask him what is bothering him. I had no time to do so tonight, for I was put to hem stitching the torn bottom of my blue skirt. I was not to quit, said Rudine, until she approved every inch. I stitched until my fingers hurt and everyone was ready to retire. Rudine came to my room and said, "Finish in the morning. I cannot believe neither your mother nor mine have seen fit to raise you in the ways of a proper gentlewoman."

I am supposed to be asleep, but I am sitting in the front room on my mattress—which I sewed myself and stuffed with straw—with the lantern burning low beside me. I can see a dark reflection in the glass. I'm glad I can't see it well, for I am beginning to cry. My eyes burn and my cheeks are hot. The scars on my arms tug and ache. I must do my crying now, for I shall not let anyone else see these tears. They didn't bring my mother and father back, and they will not change my circumstances. Only I can do that. Only Stephen and me together.

Thank God for Stephen. Thank God he is here and he understands. I can't imagine having this burden to bear on my own.

—Susanne Annalee Blackburn

6

May 8, 1863; 3:00 a.m.
My Dear Sister,

I know it will be hard for you to understand, but this is my goodbye to you, at least for now. I have decided to enlist in the army, and by the time you read this letter I will be well on my way. Marshall Fenwick and I have made a pact that we shall join together and serve our country to the best of our abilities. I believe it is what I have to do. I believe it's the best thing for everybody.

It's plain to see that Uncle Silas, Aunt Darcy, and Aunt Rudine don't understand my feelings, or yours either. They treat us like we were simple-minded tots when in reality you are most of the way to being a woman and I a man, and when I join the army, that's what I will be—a man. There comes a time when a person has to make his own choice. This is my choice, to become a soldier.

I have heard I shall make about sixteen dollars a month as a private. I promise to send all the pay I can spare back to you, so that you all can live as comfortably as possible. Insist that the aunts let you ride into town for the mail—promise to use the sidesaddle and

Aunt Rudine might let you go—and do not let the others see the money. This is what I can do for you, Susanne. I wish it were more.

Simon is old enough do a lot of the work that I've done over the years. Why, when I was his age, I did twice what he does now! I know he takes more kindly to you than he does to me, so I think with your influence he will be able to take my place in a lot of ways. In between the schooling Rudine insists on providing for him at home, with his fancy books and fancy paper and pencils, the boy could do well to learn how to do a bit of manual labor.

To be honest, dear sister, I don't think I ever want to come back to the farm or Gettysburg again. The place has been nothing but pain for me, and I think for you too. There is a huge and wonderful world waiting out there, and going to war may be a strange way to find it, but I believe that's what I will do. I will meet many people from many places and I know that in one day in the army I will learn more than all I have ever learned from Uncle Silas and Aunt Darcy.

This is what I must do, and I hope you will understand and not despise me for my decision.

My friend Marshall and I will be meeting long before the sun comes up. When you find this I will probably be wearing the uniform of the Union, and I will be very proud. I hope you will be proud of me, too.

I love you very much. I hope to live to see you again.

Your loving brother,
Stephen

7

SUSANNE STOOD, DUMBFOUNDED, clutching the letter she had found placed in her shoe sometime during the night. She had slipped her foot inside and felt the paper, then drew it out after Aunt Rudine and Aunt Darcy had gone downstairs. It was from Stephen, saying he was running away with Marshall to enlist with the Union Army.

"Uncle Silas and the aunts don't know he's gone," she said to herself as she sank into the chair at Aunt Darcy's sewing table. "They will pitch a fit that he's gone! Who is going to hunt deer? We've got but three cows now, and two are for milk and cheese. We can't eat them, heaven's knows, and need the venison! Who is to help me repair the stretch of fence by the road? I can drive a nail but can't easily lift a board. Stephen believes that Simon can learn to do the heavy chores? Oh, and cows fly and horses sing! He is too small, too sniveling, too, too . . ." She clenched her fists in her lap. She suddenly found it hard to breath. "Damn the boy! What was he thinking? Leaving us this way? What was he thinking, leaving me alone with them?"

"Susanne!" called Aunt Rudine from downstairs.

"Your uncle needs help with his pan and linens! We've breakfast! We've got much to do, child!"

On shaky legs, Susanne stood and carried the shoe and the note to the window. Outside, the land was waking with the sun, and streaked with fingers of orange and gold. To the right she could see the corner of the cornfield, newly tilled by Stephen and the mule just several days ago, and ready for the late spring planting. The lilacs were losing their brilliant purple, giving way to the delicate green of the new leaves on the branches. The wash Susanne had hung out the evening before waved like grand flags near the front walk. The window was pushed up slightly from the sill and the air that poured through was warm. Unlike the blood in Susanne's arms, which had gone cold.

"What am I to do now?" Susanne whispered. Then, she whirled around and hurled the shoe across the room, where it crashed into Aunt Darcy's sewing table and fell to the floor, taking a paper of pins and the sheers with it. "What am I supposed to do?"

Downstairs, Uncle Silas was propped up against his pillow, running his finger along the page of his open Bible. He read aloud a passage about slavery as Susanne walked past him into the kitchen, jabbing his finger at the page and swearing that God meant for some men to be the legally owned servants of other men. "Slavery is allowed by God," he said. "This war is a waste and a travesty. The South wants to be left alone to mind their business and their finance, and not told what to do by national laws voted on by the North and West! You hear me?"

"Yes," said Susanne.

Aunt Rudine and Great Aunt Darcy were leaning over the small kitchen table, up to their elbows in dusty flour, pounding dough. Simon was seated on a stool near the cookstove, whittling a poplar stick. Tiny wood shavings were curled around his feet.

"Oh, isn't that fine and productive?" Susanne said

under her breath. Aunt Rudine looked up.

"What was that? Your hair looks dreadful," she said.

Susanne touched her head. She found a tangle of braids that had not been tended to since she went to bed. "I forgot to comb it," she said.

"How can a lady forget her appearance?"

Aunt Darcy said, "Oh, mustn't forget such things, no, no, no." Her head tilted and her mouth drew up in concern.

Susanne felt her head begin to spin. Her mouth tasted of brine. She closed her eyes tightly, and beneath her, the floor seemed to shake.

"What is wrong with you?" asked Simon. "Looks like you're going to cry."

A buzzing grew in Susanne's ear. She thought, *I am going to faint. I have never fainted before.*

The voices in the kitchen faded, and became distant as the shaking of the floor became more intense and the burring in her ear got louder.

"Susanne?"

"What is this? Are you ill?"

"Susanne? Answer me!"

But then Susanne clenched her fists and drew back her head, drawing in a long breath. *No!* She thought. *I've not fainted and I will never faint. That is for silly ladies with empty heads and weak bodies, not me!* Her eyes snapped open. She grabbed hold of the table's edge and squeezed her eyes shut to clear the stars from her vision.

"Susanne?" It was Aunt Darcy.

"I'm fine," Susanne declared, looking at her aunt. "Nothing's wrong. Now, I've got linens. And then eggs."

"And your hair, child . . . ," began Aunt Rudine.

"Of course," said Susanne. "My hair. Don't worry. Everything will be done in a timely manner." She turned on her heel and went back into the parlor. Putting her arm around her uncle's shoulder, she helped push him over to his side. The sheet was soiled terribly, and the acid fume of urine overwhelming. She grit her teeth, tugged the sheet off half of the mattress, then rolled the old man back over and yanked the sheet off completely.

I don't know what I'm going to do, she thought, feeling the tightening of her neck; feeling tears burning behind her eyes yet blinking them back fiercely. *I am alone now. Stephen is gone. I must figure out what to do. I can figure it out. God help me figure it out.*

A wicker basket filled with other clothes ready to be washed was sitting by the back door. Susanne stuffed the stinky sheet into the basket.

"And the bedpan?" said Aunt Darcy. "My, my, that would not be right to forget the pan."

"Can't Simon just . . . ," she began, but then knew that even if Rudine agreed for Simon to empty the bedpan, she did not want him with her right now. And so she got the bedpan from the parlor, and, dragging the basket beside her, took them both outside. As she walked down the path, the kitchen window squealed open behind her and Aunt Rudine called, "Stephen was up before all of us. Made nary a sound! Stop by the barn and tell him to finish feeding those animals and get back to the house. I have a list of chores for him, and need him to get to them right away."

What do I say? Susanne thought as she left the basket of dirty clothes by the washtub in the yard and took the side path to the privy. And so she said nothing. Soon enough the family would realize that Stephen had abandoned them.

And it took little time for Stephen's absence to be noticed. It was during breakfast, while the family was gathered around plates of fried venison, biscuits, and bowls of apple butter and oatmeal at the table in the parlor. The front window open letting in air and flies, which were driving Simon to distraction. The conversation between the aunts centered on the need for the ladies of Adams County to continue to provide for the need of the men in the army, and the women scheduled to arrive at mid-day to cut and roll bandages to send to the front. The war had been going on for two years, and certainly, Aunt Rudine chimed, it would be over by Christmas. But until then, busy hands should help from the home front. Chat, chat, chat, with Aunt Darcy intermittently wiping the handle of her silverware with her napkin in order. Knife, spoon, fork. Knife, spoon, fork. Susanne could barely swallow her oatmeal.

Suddenly, Uncle Silas pounded his fist on the table and demanded, "And just what has become of Stephen? Where is that boy? Is one of the horses ailing? Have the rabbits escaped their hutch? Did he find the mule with founder?" The old man stared at Susanne. Aunt Rudine and Aunt Darcy ceased their chatter, and even Simon paused in his relentless efforts to keep the flies off his food.

"Father, dear," said Aunt Rudine, putting her hand on his arm. "Don't upset yourself. You aren't well."

"Susanne, tell me!" roared Uncle Silas.

"Tell you what?" asked Susanne. "Sir?"

"That's impertinent," said Rudine. "Watch your tongue!"

"Where *is* your brother?" asked Uncle Silas.

Susanne could not lie. She could withhold the truth, but she could not lie. And so she said, "Gone."

Almost in unison, the two aunts said, "Gone?"

"He's joined the army. He's off to fight for the Union."

Spoons clattered to the table top. Simon gasped. Aunt Rudine's expression for the briefest second surprised Susanne; it was one of true fear and panic, but then it shifted immediately to unmasked irritation.

"When? Why?" demanded Uncle Simon. "Who gave him permission to go?"

"No one," said Susanne. "He said it was time he became a man and made his own decisions."

"Oh, he told you he was off, did he?" said Uncle Silas. "And you said not a word to us?"

"He . . . ," began Susanne, but then she stopped herself, for if she said she had a note, they would demand to read it. And there were things there she didn't want them to see. "He let me know this morning. I was hoping he was teasing, and hiding somewhere to fool us."

Simon wiped his mouth, coughed around his food, and blurted out, "I thought he would do that! I thought he would enlist! He and Marshall were talking in whispers yesterday when we were in town."

Aunt Darcy drew her napkin to her lips and stared at the table top. Her white brows were knit together over her watery eyes. Uncle Silas sputtered and shook his head in exasperation. Aunt Rudine was the first to come to her senses. "So," she said, her prim lips pursed and one eyebrow raised in a pointy V. "The boy's gone. Lied about his age and joined the army. I supposed, then, we shall do without him. I've done without before."

"Oh, dear," mumbled Aunt Darcy. "He's gone, is he?"

"Simon's still here," offered Susanne, "he can do the work Stephen did. Simon's old enough to work in the fields. It would be good for him, really, too—"

But the moment she spoke she could see it wasn't what Rudine wanted to hear. The woman drew up in her chair and she said, "I know what my son can and cannot do. I will decide what he shall and shall not do. You do not know his fragile health, and so I would have you keep your thoughts to yourself. And as to Stephen, he is gone. I pray God he faces no harm. We shall roll a bandage for him and say a prayer, but that is all we can do."

It took every ounce of strength for Susanne to sit through the rest of the breakfast in silence. Her toes danced anxiously within the confines of her shoes, and the muscles of her arms twitched uncontrollably. No one seemed to care that Stephen was gone.

I am so alone, Susanne thought woefully.

Breakfast over, Uncle Silas was helped back to his bed, the dishes were cleared and washed, Simon went off to several of the simple chores of which his mother thought him capable—taking food scraps to the chickens, collecting the dried clothes from the line, cleaning the ash from the bottom of the Dutch oven and dumping it over the vegetable garden. Aunt Darcy, Aunt Rudine, and Susanne spent the next hour preparing for the guests who were to arrive at noon.

Across the front hall from the parlor was a room never used, a dining room at one time, which usually had its door closed tightly. Susanne had only peeked in once or twice since she and Stephen had come to Sycamore Grove, for it was useless and nearly empty, boasting only a fireplace, a settee with well-worn velvet upholstery, and a red and blue threadbare Oriental. Uncle Silas had said they'd sold most of the nice furniture, the silver sets, and most of the wall adornments when Aunt Darcy went crazy and he'd grown ill.

The room was draped in cobwebs and littered with gray dust balls which fluttered before Susanne's footsteps like rabbits running for cover. Armed with a mop and a bucket of soapy water, Susanne took her station at the window and then the mantle, as Rudine and Darcy tackled with polish and broom. Then the three maneuvered the large parlor table through the parlor door, across the hall, and into the dining room. Uncle Silas lay in bed grumbling that they best not nick the walls, then drifted off for his mid-morning nap. The chairs were likewise moved across the hall from the parlor. Simon watched from the stairs, seated half-way up, his face pressed between the balustrades, not making a single offer to help with the move. After a few minutes he grew bored with the spectacle, and went upstairs to the room he shared—or *had* shared—with Stephen to read.

Aunt Darcy's sewing scissors, pins, and thread were

brought down from Susanne's sleeping quarters along with the large sewing basket full of scraps the old woman had been saving to make a quilt.

Hands on hips, Aunt Rudine stood in the dining room and surveyed the offerings. "I certainly hope the other ladies bring a good bit more material than we have here. It is embarrassing to hostess an event and have so little. Why, if I'd known, Mother, I would not have left all my lovely fabrics back in New Jersey. I had silk, satin, and of course, cotton. Cotton is best for bandages. What we have is pitiful. It would barely bind up a dog and a bugler."

"Oh, dear," said Aunt Darcy. "We don't have much, do we?"

"No," continued Aunt Rudine. "But perhaps we can make up for it with something tasty to offer our company."

"What did you offer ladies at your home?" asked Aunt Darcy. It was clear the idea of so many visitors had her nervous. Her voice was pinched, her oft-worried face was drawn up all the more, making it seem as if her thin skin might just rip for being touched. She began to gather the lace at the end of one sleeve into three little folds, then let it out again. Fold, release. Fold, release. She'd not entertained the entire time Susanne and Stephen had lived there. "What did you dine on? What was fitting and proper when ladies visited you?"

Rudine went to the mirror that hung over the mantle, and began rubbing it vigorously with a cloth to remove the years'-long grime that clung there. "Mother," she said tersely. "Don't you recall what we served guests when I was younger? I can't believe you have forgotten. You taught me all I know and now. . . ." She turned around to face the old woman. Susanne watched the scene between the two. Until now, Aunt Rudine had tolerated her mother's strange behaviors and timidity. But it seemed that was not going to be the case much longer. "Now must I instruct you like a little girl? What has happened to you since last we saw each other?"

Great Aunt Darcy's mouth fell open. She stammered, "Rudine, dear, what do you mean?"

"It is not simple senility, Mother. I've seen senility, and that is not what ails you. For you understand things, you know what we are saying. Yet you refuse to go outside to simply hang a blouse on the line or to take a stroll in the yard or garden! You repeat actions over and over until I'm quite ready to pull my hair from my head! What is it? Tell me! I can bare it no longer!"

Susanne watched Aunt Darcy fall to the settee. Tears swam in the woman's eyes as if she'd been slapped. For the first time Susanne could remember, she felt a desire to protect the old woman. Yes, she was slow and confused, but she was never unkind. Not the way her daughter and husband were.

"Why don't we go to the kitchen and bake the cookies?" asked Susanne.

Rudine ignored her. "Will you tell me, Mother? Before this day goes any longer? Before I can no longer bear the uncertain? Have I lost my mother as well as my husband?"

"It was the slave!" came Silas' gruff voice from the parlor. "It was the damnable slave she took in!"

Aunt Darcy gasped. "Silas, no more! Leave it alone!"

"Mother!" insisted Rudine.

Darcy put her hands over her eyes and burst into sobs. Her frail body heaved, and her prim hat was knocked from her head and dangled there by a single hair pin.

Susanne went to her great-aunt and put her arm tentatively around the woman's shoulder. She'd never hugged her before and the move felt awkward.

"Mother!" said Rudine.

" 'Twas the slave!" Uncle Silas called again. "She found her and invited her to stay for a while. 'Oh, just for a while,' she promised me. Just until—"

"No!" cried Aunt Darcy, throwing her hands up like

an itinerant preacher at a camp meeting. "Say no more, I can't bear it!"

There was a knock on the door. Susanne looked at Rudine, who jerked her head, indicating Susanne to answer. Susanne gave her aunt's shoulder the gentlest of squeezes, then went to the front hall. With a yank on the knob, the door creaked open. There stood Marjorie Olson's mother and her sister-in-law, Jolene Anderson. Mrs. Olson was dressed in pale yellow and Mrs. Anderson in deep navy and white. Each wore a snood, gloves, and carried bundles and satchels. On the lane beyond the gate, the carriage which had brought them was turning around to leave.

"Good morning, Susanne!" said Mrs. Olson. She was a pretty woman, with blonde hair and dark green eyes like Marjorie. "We thought we would come a bit early and see if we could help prepare for the gathering."

From the dining room, Susanne could hear Aunt Darcy still sobbing. The ladies at the door heard it as well, and looked at each other and then Susanne. "Has someone been harmed, sweet Jesus?" Mrs. Olson asked. "Is someone ill?"

"No," said Susanne, stepping aside to let the ladies in their wide skirts into the front hall. "Aunt Darcy's just . . . upset."

The ladies looked at each other, and Susanne could read their thoughts.

The old woman is crazy, of course. Such a pity.

They went into the dining room and Susanne followed. Aunt Rudine had poised herself beside her mother at the settee, trying to look as though she were comforting her.

"Dears!" exclaimed Mrs. Olson. "What is the trouble? How can we help?" She kneeled in front of Aunt Darcy and Mrs. Anderson took Aunt Darcy's hand carefully. "Did she have a fright, Rudine? A pain?"

"Oh, it was but a mouse!" said Aunt Rudine, and Susanne looked at her sharply. "We were having the best of times, laughing and moving the table about for the best sunlight, and there across her foot scurried a mouse! But don't worry, we've caught it and are rid of it."

The ladies laughed, and consoled Aunt Darcy, who sat without saying a word except, "Thank you, thank you."

Susanne glared at Aunt Rudine. She'd not known the woman to lie before. And to save her own face, so no one would know it was she who had brought her elderly mother to tears.

The two ladies had brought a bundle of cotton cloth and a satchel of small meat pies. As Aunt Darcy retired to her bedroom to regain herself, the others went into the kitchen to roll out and bake almond cookies and apple tarts. As the hour passed, other neighbor ladies arrived, dressed for the occasion and bearing sacks and bundles of cloth. By noon, the tarts and cookies were cooling in the kitchen window and the ladies had settled themselves in the dining room around the table.

Before they began their civic duty, Mrs. Olson asked if she could say a prayer for the army, and the ladies all bowed their heads.

"Almighty Father," she said softly. "whose providence watcheth over all things and in whose hands is the disposal of all events, we look to thee for the protection and blessing of those men who have gone forth in battle. Bear them up in thine arms as they struggle to win the good fight, the fight to bring our ailing nation back to unity."

"Yes, dear Lord," whispered Mrs. Randolph, whose brother was fighting.

"Please, my God," said Mrs. Devonshire, whose son had died last winter not of a battle wound but of a fever contracted in camp.

"Protect them, dear Lord," prayed Mrs. Olson, "and let them be neither harmed by terrors that fly by night nor arrows that fly by day. Give your angels charge over them and keep them in all thy ways. In Christ Jesus' name we pray. Amen."

"Amen," said the ladies.

"Amen," said Susanne. As the other ladies picked up their needles and threads and began cutting and stitching lengths of cloth into bandages to be rolled and sent to the front, Susanne could only stare at the piece in her hands, an irregular block of cloth covered with a silly floral print.

He might be shot, she thought incredulously. *He might be wounded and crippled in the war.* Since finding his note this morning, her concern had been for her own welfare, for her own misery at the hands of her bizarre family. And she hadn't yet spared a moment to consider the dire danger her brother was facing. *Why, he might even be killed! Heavenly Father, will he survive this war?*

Susanne was vaguely aware of the conversation around her. Someone was saying that although the Union had taken a beating, it would come back strong, and soon. Surely it was the Lord's will that the North be victorious. Someone else was saying that she'd planted an entire garden of beans for the army, a near acre it was, and soon the harvest would be shipped to the good men, wherever they were fighting. Someone else mentioned that Silas certainly did seem to enjoy his napping, for his snoring was audible from across the hall. There were several light giggles around the table.

Slowly, Susanne picked up a needle and ran the eye through with thread, then found a suitable scrap of cloth to stitch to it for a good-sized bandage. *This is for you,* she thought. *Stephen, I pray you will not need it, that you will never need it, but it is for you.*

8

STEPHEN'S THROAT WAS painfully dry as he stood before the wooden recruitment table on the grass in front of Gettysburg's courthouse. His shoulders were cramped from waiting in line. His face, freshly scrubbed with well water in the pre-dawn hours, was now coated heavily with dust. And his hair, which had been carefully combed before he had sneaked away from the farmhouse, was now tussled and tangled from the sporadic breezes along Baltimore Street.

It was late morning. The sun, which had just been a red smudge on the hills to the east of town when Stephen and Marshall arrived, now held the center of the sky, and glared down upon the gathering in the courthouse grass.

The recruiting sergeant had just arrived with a grumbling and spitting, and was now seated behind the table, sorting out papers. He wore a blue uniform and a scowl, as if someone had already perturbed him, and he hadn't even begun his morning task. The sergeant's assistant, a boy of perhaps eighteen in a well-worn blue jacket and trousers, stood at attention behind the table, waiting for something to do. A third uniformed man stood at the right side of the table with his arms crossed. Stephen chewed on the inside of his cheek to keep the rest of his body calm. He was first in line. He didn't like that.

"What's the bloody wait?" Marshall whispered in Stephen's ear. He was directly behind his friend. Behind Marshall a few other men and boys had taken their place in the line. "It's not that there are a hoard of us to enlist! Why, most able-bodied men of Adams County are already wearing the uniform and are off fighting rebels in the south."

"Shhh," whispered Stephen over his shoulder.

The sergeant continued to dig through his stack of papers. He jerked his head at the young assistant, who took a well of ink and pen from a haversack at his waist, and put them both on the table. He uncapped the well, then stood back, again at attention.

"Come on, come on," hissed Marshall.

"Shhhh," urged Stephen.

Stephen and Marshall had arrived in town at the crack of dawn on their horses, which they'd left hitched outside the tannery with a letter for Mr. Bowler asking if he'd see that they were returned safely home.

"Name!" shouted the sergeant.

Stephen flinched slightly, and stepped closer to the table.

"Stephen Alan Blackburn . . . sir."

"Residence?"

"Sycamore Grove farm, Adam's County, a few miles up Harrisburg Road."

"Age?"

"Eighteen . . . nearly nineteen," Stephen said in a raspy voice. It had been a lot easier to say to himself, or to Marshall. They had practiced on the way.

The sergeant's dark eyes narrowed and studied him intently. Stephen tried not to shrink from the gaze. "You don't look any eighteen years old."

"I am. My birthday is, ah, August 19. . . ." He paused

for a minute, desperately trying to think. "That would be 1844."

"Until you're twenty years old you still need parental consent to enlist."

Stephen felt his face beginning to burn. Behind him, he heard Marshall whisper something he couldn't understand. Then the words became clear to him.

"I want to be a bugler, sir."

"What's that?"

"I said I want to be a bugler."

The man raised one eyebrow. His assistant tried to suppress a smile. Stephen wondered if that boy had gotten into the army the same way. "You want to be a bugler?"

"Yes, sir. Indeed I do."

"And you play the bugle?"

"The bugle is a fine instrument. One of my favorites."

"I see," said the sergeant. "Hmm. Buglers don't shoot. Don't need to meet the same age requirement. Lucky for you, I'd say. Can you write?"

"Oh, yes, sir."

"We need a bit of a check first before you sign. Step there, sharply, to Mr. Lee."

"Certainly, sir."

Stephen glanced back at Marshall, who bore an expression of combined cheer and caution. Stephen's own stomach was rippling uncomfortably with nervousness.

The man was a surgeon, and all business. "Yes, I'm Lee," he barked as Stephen stood before him, "but no relation to that Southern traitor, and don't say another word about it! Heart!" Stephen quickly unbuttoned his shirt, pulled his suspenders from his shoulders, and let the shirt fall open. Surgeon Lee pressed his ear to several places on Stephen's chest, and then gave a satisfied nod. He then had Stephen open his mouth and glanced at his teeth and tongue, and then pulled his eyelids up and down to have a look.

"All right then," the surgeon said, standing straight.

"You seem in better shape than some. No invalid here. Sign your name."

Stephen took the pen from the ink well and, trying hard not to let his hand tremble too greatly, signed his name on the otherwise empty enlistment roll. When he put the pen back he realized his name was completely illegible.

"All right, Mr. Blarthbunn, for the bugle corps, you will go around the courthouse and stand by the second boxwood. Not the first. The first is the line for armed privates. The second for buglers and drummers. You got that?"

"Yes, sir."

The sergeant dismissed him with a wave of his hand, and Stephen hurried around the building. As he turned the corner, he saw two short lines of men. He'd assumed he would be first, but likely the sergeant and his assistants had come to Gettsyburg last night and had done a little late-night recruiting over their beers and their ninepins. Three uniformed soldiers stood by the lines, looking dignified and giving directions to the new enlistees. The sergeant had told Stephen to get in the second line—which he saw was composed of just a few very young boys. And here, he realized, was his opportunity. Instead of getting in line with the children, he fell in behind the last man in the first line.

"In for the infantry, huh?" said the man in front of him, who appeared to be well over twenty years old, stocky and powerfully built.

"Yeah," Stephen said. "I can sure shoot a gun and I'm ready to shoot me some rebels."

The other young man chuckled. "I'm hoping to get assigned to the artillery. I've seen a Howitzer go off before. A shot from one of those could blow up this whole post office."

"There you are," came a familiar voice, and Stephen turned to see Marshall falling in behind him. "Simple!"

"So far."

A moment later, a burly officer with bright red hair stepped up in front of the group of young men and called out, "I want everybody to raise his right hand to be sworn in. All right, repeat after me, 'I . . . say your name . . . ,'' the man paused while each man spoke his name, ". . . do solemnly swear to faithfully defend and preserve the Constitution of these United States." As the passage was repeated, the officer continued, "I hereby swear that I enter into this agreement of my own free will and without obligation to any other individual or government." Again he paused. And then, to conclude: "I hereby pledge my service to the United States Army and will abide by all its rules, policies, and judgments for a period of no less than three years, so help me God."

Stephen found his voice had not risen above a whisper. But he had done it. And now, the red-haired officer said, "You, buglers and drummers, wait to be called. You!" He pointed to the group that included Stephen. "Over to those wagons. You'll be taken to drill camp, outfitted, and fed. Welcome to the United States Army, soldiers!"

And so began Stephen's term of service. He and Marshall boarded one of the wagons, as instructed, where they were packed in with the other young recruits. The wagons set off down the road and out of town—an uncomfortable, tedious ride—to the drill camp in east rural Adams County. Stephen knew the first few miles, but then the land became unfamiliar. He sat with his legs crossed beside Marshall, and joked with the others about the fact that now the Southerners would see some real fighting. But all the while, he wondered what Susanne was doing, and wishing Uncle Silas could see him now.

The camp was a wide area of fenced land, filled with what looked like an ocean of canvas tents. Stephen saw a large number of men in uniform marching around the perimeter under the instruction of a shouting drill sergeant. The soldiers must have been new, Stephen thought, for their ranks were only a shade better than disorderly.

"Don't they look shabby?" Marshall said, echoing Stephen's thoughts. "We'll do better in our sleep."

Stephen nodded.

The wagon pulled up to the center of the compound, where the American flag flew proudly from a tall wooden staff. A blue-coated soldier stood waiting for them, his face red and swollen, probably from prolonged exposure to the sun. His muscles bulged even through his dusty uniform, and his eyes looked cunning as he watched the new recruits arrive. As the other wagons pulled in behind them, Stephen hopped out, glad to stretch his legs, with Marshall following behind him.

"Troops!" called the man in a deep, grating voice. "Assemble in front of the Stars and Stripes in two lines. Got that? Two lines! Hop to it! Hop to it!"

Stephen hustled into position as the other recruits fell in on either side of him, and in the shuffle, he found that Marshall was no longer beside him. He looked anxiously for his friend, only to see him in the row behind him, several feet away.

"Ten-hut!" called the drill sergeant. Stephen went rigidly to attention, noting that some of the other recruits seemed to follow their orders with considerably less alacrity. Seeing that a fellow a few men down appeared to be slouching, the sergeant stalked up to him and shouted directly into the young man's face, "Soldier, do you know what it means to stand at attention? Stand up, shoulders back! Chin up! Eyes straight ahead! What are you looking at? Don't you look at me!"

The sergeant's exaggerated manner tickled Stephen's funny bone, and he could not stop himself from laughing a little. Suddenly, he found himself the focus of the sergeant's ire, for the huge, swelling face rushed up to his. Stephen could smell onions on the man's breath. "You find something funny, private? You like to laugh at another man's mistakes? If you do, you've made a big mistake yourself, and I can assure you, no one will find that funnier than me. Do you think I'm joking with you, soldier?"

"No!" Stephen said, his voice quivering. "Sorry, sir!"

"That's 'I'm sorry, sergeant!' Can I hear you say that?"

"I'm sorry, sergeant!"

"Now," boomed the man's voice as he stepped away from Stephen. "That's lesson number one. You're all in this together. No one will laugh at the failure of any other man. You're going to be working as a team. Does anyone here have a problem with that?"

"No, sir!" Stephen called, hoping to improve his standing in the sergeant's eyes.

"And you reply, 'Sergeant, no, sergeant,' or 'Sergeant, yes, sergeant.' Is that clear?"

"Sergeant, yes, sergeant!" came a reply, almost in unison.

"Again!"

"Sergeant, yes, sergeant!" This time, the response was loud and harmonious.

"My name, if it's any concern of yours, is Drill Sergeant Charles Lawson. For the next few weeks, I am the only person to look after you. You don't talk without my permission. You don't eat without my permission. You don't sleep without my permission. You don't yawn, belch, fart, sneeze, cough, or breathe without my permission. Is that perfectly clear?"

"Sergeant, yes, sergeant!" Stephen cried, as did the rest of the company.

"Our first exercise is to march over to that tent there, where you will be fitted for uniforms. You will wear your uniform proudly. Once you are in that uniform, you are going to become the best damn soldiers this country can produce. You're going to be fighting men, and you're going to march and march, and when you're done marching, you're going to march some more. Then you are going to kick some rebel hindquarters so far south that even the penguins won't be able to find them. Does that sound good to you men?"

And now, every man in the assembly cried out loud and strong, "Sergeant, yes, sergeant!"

"This is a Springfield rifle," bellowed Sergeant Lawson. He stood before the company of now-uniformed young troops, holding up a gleaming, polished steel gun—just like the one that each of the men now carried at his shoulder. "It is your .58 caliber, rifled-barrel, muzzle-loading friend to end all friends. You will break down this weapon, reassemble this weapon, drill with this weapon, and sleep with this weapon. But until I say when, you will not shoot this weapon. Ammunition is a commodity reserved for the troops on the line. Until you are on the line, you will learn all there is to know about the operation of this exceptional Springfield product."

The sergeant then held up a long, wicked-looking blade which he affixed to the barrel of the rifle. "Now. This is your bayonet. Your bayonet is your little helper when you get close enough to Johnny Reb to poke his eyes out. Remember, a Rebel doesn't care that you look just like his precious little brother or that you and he might've gone to the same church when you were babies. He will poke you and think nothing of it. Therefore, it is your duty to adjust the rebel's attitude by killing him. Is that very clear?"

"Sergeant, yes, sergeant!" Stephen cried, his blood pumping. The morning was warm, and the uniform was heavy, causing him to sweat uncomfortably. But the heavy solidity of the weapon in his hands and the energy-charged atmosphere filled him with more vitality and sense of purpose than he could ever remember feeling. He could see the same sentiment reflected in Marshall's eyes as his friend watched the sergeant disassemble the musket with quick, expert hands.

Two days had passed in the camp, and so far, the fresh recruits had mostly marched, marched, and marched some more, at first empty handed, and then with long sticks meant to simulate a rifle. Stephen had the beginnings of a prickly beard, which made him feel all the more a man, a soldier. The days had been long and tiring, and they had only meager food: a few ounces of dried beef, some pork, rice, bread, beans, and water. Much of the local meat and produce they might have otherwise enjoyed was being sent to the widely dispersed army units, but even the active troops often found themselves short of food and had to scavenge. At least, that was what Stephen had heard from some of the young men whose family or friends had already taken part in the fighting.

"The beauty of this rifle is that its parts are interchangeable," growled the sergeant. "If you are fighting and a component of your weapon fails, it can be replaced by a component from one of your dead friend's weapons. Wipe that frown off your face, soldier, this is war."

Stephen could barely refrain from chuckling, for he still found he could barely take the sergeant's bluster seriously. But he knew Sergeant Lawson would take exception to such an idea, and Stephen didn't care to have that powerful onion breath in his face again. So, he maintained a stern demeanor and continued to watch with interest as the sergeant deftly reassembled the trigger, hammer and percussion cap components of the rifle.

And now, as happened so often that it seemed to be old habit, the sergeant hollered, "Now, fall into marching order! Shoulder arms! Hop to it! Hop to it!"

Stephen turned to his right, and quickly stepped into the forming line two paces behind the man in front of him. This much had become second nature, for the sergeant had begun hammering the formation drill into them from the moment they had donned their uniforms.

But now, Stephen was actually carrying his rifle—ten pounds of extra weight to which he was unaccustomed. And soon, he knew, they would be marching in full gear—their bedrolls, their knapsacks of clothing and personal items, rations—all meant to build up endurance. Even young and strong as most of the men were, this kind of exertion was taxing. Stephen was fortunate to be well-conditioned from his active life on the farm.

Marshall joined the line right behind Stephen. "This is going to get old fast," he whispered. "I want to shoot this rifle, no matter what the sergeant says."

"No talking in the ranks!" Sergeant Lawson barked. "What did I tell you about opening your mouth without permission?" The stocky, brutish man lumbered up to Marshall and leaned down into his face. "Yes, soldier, I can hear a fly buzzing at the other end of the camp, so don't look so surprised! Now let's get marching!"

And Stephen had to choke back a laugh, for as the column began to move, Sergeant Lawson raised a fist and thumped Marshall on the head, just as Stephen had often thumped his cousin Simon.

But after two solid hours of marching back and forth, and up and down, Stephen's feet in the stiff Brogan boots were stinging fiercely. His throat was parched and the rifle pressing against his shoulder had begun to chafe. His strength was still holding out, but some of the young men around him were beginning to falter. As the company completed what Stephen hoped would be the final circuit before breaking for their afternoon meal, he saw the sergeant eyeing the stragglers with abject disapproval. And as they trudged up to the main gate of the camp, instead of ordering a halt, Sergeant Lawson cried, "You girls have not yet begun to march. We're going for another round, double time, double time!"

Stephen now felt his anger beginning to rise. Invigorated though he felt, he could scarcely contain his resentment toward orders that seemed unreasonable. Uncle Silas had often demanded the unreasonable of

Stephen. Before he even realized it, he blurted out, "Sergeant, couldn't we stop and at least have a drink of water first?"

Surprisingly, Sergeant Lawson did not even turn his head to look at him. Instead, he called out, "Corporal Jennings!"

A moment later, one of the young men who helped keep order in the ranks stepped up to the sergeant and went to attention. "Sergeant?"

"I'm told I'm to allow the company to break for water and afternoon chow. We will begin drilling again at 0200 hours. Oh, except for young private Blackburn there. Take that man out and drill him like hell until the rest of the men have finished eating."

"Sergeant, yes, sergeant!" cried Corporal Jennings, who then turned to Stephen with an expression of both amusement and sympathy. He smiled to reveal straight white teeth and his blue eyes narrowed as he stepped up and leaned into Stephen's face. "Soldier! Ten-hut!"

With a silent groan of disbelief, Stephen snapped to attention, thrusting the butt of his rifle to the ground. He kept his eyes straight ahead, keeping his gaze averted from either the corporal or the sergeant's mirth-filled eyes.

"Shoulder arms!" chanted the corporal. "Forward . . . march! Double time, double time!"

Stephen picked up his feet and set off, hearing the relieved groans of the other men as they fell out of formation. He knew Marshall was watching him with eyes full of pity.

What a long day this is going to be, he thought morosely. The only consolation, he decided, was that when the corporal got up in his face, he didn't smell of onions.

The evening meal was scarcely any more satisfying than midday chow. A bit of hardtack, some bread three-quarters of the way to stale, a few ounces of boiled beans, and an apple, all blessed heartily by the chaplain as if it was a banquet. Already Stephen thought he had lost two pounds from the lean fare and the constant drilling. But once the sun went down and until they turned in at 0830 hours, the men were left to entertain themselves as they pleased.

Marshall and Stephen found themselves sitting with a group of young men around a roaring fire, listening to the stories some of them had to tell. Many of the men were from the surrounding vicinity, though quite a few had come from distant towns to join up. A surprising number of them, Stephen found, had enlisted much for the same reason he had—to escape a life of discontentment and to seek adventure.

"I don't know nothing about no states' rights, and I give a whit about no colored man," said a lanky fellow seated on a blanket to Stephen's right. "But they ain't no future working for pennies in no Baltimore factory turning out bedsprings for rich folks. I figure I'm gonna die sooner turning them cranks than going off to fight." The young man smiled, revealing crooked, yellowed teeth.

"Same thing working on a farm," Marshall said, chewing on the tip of a blade of grass. His mustache had been combed and twisted into points with spit. Stephen thought it looked dandy. He hoped to have his own soon. "I guess being in the army's a hard life. But at least it's got honor in it. We got a reason to be doing what we're doing. Back home, there's just nothing to look forward to except old age. That's why me and my friend Stephen joined up."

"Yeah," Stephen said. "Back home I just take orders from the old folks. 'Stephen do this, Stephen go there.' I got no say in anything. This, I'm doing it for me and my country. I figure it's gotta be more exciting than just wasting away. But if my great-aunt and -uncle had known I was enlisting, I'd be just as dead as if I'd been shot by a Rebel."

A few of the young men laughed. Then, a familiar, baritone voice from behind him said, "So, Private Blackburn . . . you and Private Fenwick are good friends?"

Stephen turned to see the somber eyes of Corporal Jennings studying him, his face turned flickering gold by the firelight. "That's right, Corporal. Been friends ever since I moved to Adams County four years ago."

Corporal Jennings nodded thoughtfully. And to Stephen's surprise, the young man laid a gentle hand on his shoulder. "My best advice then, is that you take a different assignment from your friend when you're sent up."

Stephen frowned. "Why do you say that?"

Everyone fell silent as the Corporal stared momentarily into the firelight. "Because a war is no place for friends, Stephen. I had a good friend, too, before I came to this place. We were at Antietam, just last fall. I saw it happen. He standing there with me, not any farther than I am to you. And a cannonball splashed him to pieces. One second he was there . . . then he was gone. The only thing left of him was the blood and brain I had all over me. Worst thing I ever saw."

Not a man spoke as the corporal turned away and walked into the darkness. His voice floated eerily back to them. "You don't want to have any friends when you're in battle."

9

May 25, 1863

The house is quiet, and it is quite late, after ten. Uncle Silas is snoring downstairs. Simon has quit his tossing and turning in his room. The aunts have ceased their conversation next door.

Though I never would have admitted this at first, for I so detested this sewing room and the fact that I was ousted from my bed, I now find the room quite to my liking. I would not tell Aunt Rudine that, to be certain, for I find her so abrasive it is as if she were a washboard to skin and I have little patience for her and the insufferable Simon. Yet now that I've slept here for almost a month, I find I quite like my solitude. I no longer have to take care of my turning in the bed as to not disturb Aunt Darcy. Why, I can flip back and forth all I want and there is not a soul to complain. I can even stay up late as I am now, with my lantern turned low, and write. Or paint.

I have found that I have a talent with the brush and the watercolors. I would only write this in my journal, as to say it to anyone but paper might seem as if I were bragging. Although the flute eludes me, and my attempts at music are nothing but squeaks, I have discovered that I rather fancy making paintings of things about the farm. As long as Aunt Rudine is not hovering over me with her tedious instructions, I should amend. I've got a painting of the barn, and another of the cornfield, which is planted but poorly so. Aunt Rudine allowed Simon and me to lay seed but Simon grew weary quickly and Rudine would not have me work myself into a sweat. She said we should find a hired man to do these chores with Stephen gone. Such a waste of money that would be! I've another painting of Rock Creek with its growth of reeds and its forget-me-nots on the bank.

A third, which I've just only started, is of Aunt Darcy. She was at the kitchen window, looking out across the yard at Pratt's Woods beyond the field, and I was outside on a stone near the barn with my paints. I had not intended to paint her, but rather the path and the chickens pecking the ground, but I looked up and there she stood, her face at the glass, her eyes fixed on the far away forest. I was stunned to find that there was an illusion of sorts, much like a parlor trick of light and shadow. At one moment she seemed to be my elderly great-aunt, but the very next moment she looked as if she were a young girl. Her face was full of wonder and anticipation, of fear and hope. I found that the woman who I've thought so long as just a harmless lunatic had a strange beauty about her. I marveled, and began to paint. I have not finished, nor have I shown anyone this painting.

I received my first letter from Stephen this afternoon. It had been a full week since I had been into town with Aunt Rudine for sugar and flour, and I told her that I would be happy to ride Molly, sidesaddle of course, to purchase a new pair of shoes for Simon, as his are wearing a hole in the soles that are beyond repairing. She agreed reluctantly, saying that she would accompany me if she could, but that she had a pain in her neck and would have to stay at the farm. She sternly warned me, however, of the proper behavior of a young lady while in town. I assured her I would follow her good example.

As soon as I was clear of the farm, I urged Molly into a gallop, and I felt free and happy with the wind grabbing my hat and my skirt flapping. I passed everyone I met along the way, leaving them in a blur, and remembered how I used to beat Stephen in our silly races.

There was a letter at the post office, and I nervously put it in my pocket and bought Simon's shoes at the shop next door, then took Molly to the train station where I sat on the bench and ripped open the envelope.

"Dear God," I prayed. "Let him be safe."

The letter had been written en route to Virginia. Stephen said he was fine, still sore with some of the constant drilling, but rather bored with the routine, the tiresome rations of salt beef and beans, and ready to go into battle for the glory of the Union. Marshall was likewise fine and likewise ready to take on Rebels. There were soldiers who were sick, not from any battle wounds but from various fevers and ills, and Stephen found it surprising how many were either being treated by the company surgeon or being sent back home. "You would think you were listening to a chorus of Uncle Silases," he wrote, "with all the coughing in the tents at night!" Stephen said he was learning to play a willow flute as a fellow private was quite the musician and anxious to share his talents. Such it is! I hate the flute and Stephen enjoys it!

Inside the envelope was seven dollars.

I sat on the bench for a good many minutes, stilling my heart. Jennie Wade and her mother came by in their rig, and paused to ask if I'd had bad news. I know Stephen has a soft heart for Jennie, though I doubt she has one for him, yet her face was kind and genuinely concerned. I said it was good news, thank you, and they went on.

But now as I sit on my mattress and look out at the night sky, which is clouded now and dark gray with the veiled moon, I wonder if the next letter from Stephen will be as joyful. I know he looks forward to battle. It is not something I can understand, but for some reason, he does.

To my dearest brother, I quote the blessed word of God from Psalms. May they comfort you even as I write them.

'He shall cover thee with his feathers, and under his wings shall thou trust. His truth shall be thy shield and buckler. Thou shall not be afraid for terrors by night, nor arrows that fly by day. Nor for pestilence that walketh in darkness, nor for destruction that wasteth at noonday.'

Be safe, Stephen.

Amen.

Amen.

—Susanne Annalee Blackburn

10

Stephen Blackburn's Journal
June 14, 1863

I have decided to keep my journal during my service to my country. One day I might care to look back and see how life was when I was a soldier.

Being in the army is very different from anything I ever expected. I figured I'd be going to fight right away, but there was nothing but drilling and marching and then marching and drilling. We learned how to move in file, how to work our rifles, how to pair up with another soldier and put our single sheets of army-issue canvas together to make a two-man tent, and to do it in complete darkness. We learned how to fight with a knife, and how to build fires. The food is bad and sometimes terrible, and often it's got bugs in it. The beef has so much salt in it you've got to soak it in water before you can eat it. The only thing good is the coffee, and everyone always looks forward to getting a hot cupful. We are required to read our Army-issued prayer book every day. My father would be happy for that, at least. As to me being a soldier, I do not know if he would be happy or not.

Several fellows turned up with measles the other day, and immediately they were shipped out. We were told that sick men can wipe out an entire company if care isn't taken. A lot of illnesses that spread in camp can kill as sure as a Rebel bullet.

I felt bad for those sick men. Maybe they'll die. Maybe not. But they came to fight like we did, and won't be able to now.

Once we finished training, Marshall and I were assigned to the garrison far south at Winchester, where we figured we'd be part of a big force that would take back the State of Virginia for the Union.

Were we ever wrong.

We were to join a company as part of General Robert Milroy's army. Marshall and I were both excited to finally be off to do what we were trained to do. But I never expected to find what we found.

Our unit was composed of men of various talents with rifle and with directions, a ragtag bunch they were, some of which still didn't know how to load a gun when it was time to march south to Virginia. We took off with this bunch and with our understandably irritable officers, and a day into our march, before we had even left Pennsylvania, we heard the garrison in Winchester to which we were assigned was under attack by the Rebels and we had to hasten there as a relief force.

We picked up our pace on the road, though it was still several days' walk. Our feet burned in spite of the endless marching we'd done at our training camp and the calluses that had formed on our soles. I was thrilled and anxious. Marshall, I could tell, felt the same way. At night, as we huddled around our camp fire outside our makeshift tents, we talked with the other soldiers and imagined our impending victory. Our boys at Winchester would be glad to see us and we would save them from the Rebs. I tried to play the willow flute I'd been given by a fellow private but could barely hold my fingers on the holes to make the music. I will not allow my fingers to be so disobedient when facing the enemy, however!

As we moved farther south we saw several groups of men going northward on foot, looking suspicious and saying very little to us as we hailed to them. There was whispering along the lines that these men might be deserters. I hear that if deserters are caught, they are shot by their commanding officer. That's a more frightening thought to me than being killed by rebels—to be executed by your own side. How do you have that explained to your family? Wouldn't Uncle Silas find that to his expectation of me?

At one point yesterday I asked a fellow near me when we would reach Virginia. He said we already had. I looked about myself, at the oaks and cedars and honeysuckle vines lining the roadside, at the barns and houses and cattle, and was disappointed. Somehow, I thought the place would look different. Foreign. Unfriendly. Why, Virginia looks just like Pennsylvania!

We were closing in on Winchester this afternoon, shy of it perhaps five miles, when we heard the booming of artillery. I could see explosions. They were huge flashes of fire among the trees up ahead, and they sent up billowing columns of smoke. I figured we were about to reach the garrison and start the fighting. My blood got to racing, and my stomach twisted so hard the dried beef I'd had in the morning rushed into my mouth. There was a fight awaiting us! But I wasn't afraid. I was eager! My fingers itched to hold my gun and aim it at those Southerners!

But there wasn't any garrison, not like I thought we'd find. It was nothing but men, both standing and dead, in rows of trenches. There was mud and bugs and excrement. Whatever fighting had gone on, it was over, and traces of smoke from cannon and rifle hung like a fog over the ground. There were stands of trees around, and a big field, and on the other side was where they said *the Rebels were, but I couldn't see them.*

There were two houses nearby, and a dilapidated barn, where horse-drawn ambulances and men-born stretchers hauled the wounded for operating and tending. I couldn't tell if the houses were deserted or not; likely so, for I couldn't imagine a family hiding there in a cellar, praying for the soldiers to leave.

Thank God the fighting will never be allowed to go so far north as Gettysburg. I would hate my sister to see such terrible things.

Our soldiers here had been defeated by the Rebs, as hard as that is to write without snapping my pen in anger. The carnage was dreadful, and the wounded nearly as pitiable as the dead. I haven't ever heard grown men scream like some were. It is awful to hear. Much of the ground was charred. I recalled the burned earth beneath our home in Rhode Island, and then forced my thoughts away from it. In some places the blackened earth was puddled in scarlet, as if the ground itself had been cut and was bleeding.

Marshall and I came up to a man who was seated in the mud, clutching a crude crutch made from a tree branch. His right foot was missing. The rag around the ghastly wound was gummy with dried blood. The man saw us staring, and he told us his name was Jacob Wonderley. He'd had his foot removed just an hour ago, and as soon as a wagon could get there, he and some of the others would be taken to Washington to the train, and then sent home to his family in New York. He was clearly drunk from whiskey given him for the pain.

"You boys new?" he drawled.

Marshall and I nodded.

"Hear that?" he asked, his voice sliding up in down in his stupor. "That screaming you hear from over in that barn over there ain't from the boys being shot. Boys get shot and they moan. Scream when they get hit, yes, but then lie there and moan around in the pain. Them fresh screams, though, that's from the surgeon

taking off arms and legs that are so blown apart they can't be saved."

I looked at the barn, at Marshall, then back at Jacob.

The man continued, "They sometimes got chloroform but sometimes not. Here all we get for the pain is some liquor and a piece of cloth to bite on. I know. I was awake while the surgeon sliced through the flesh of this foot then sawed the bone in two."

I didn't want to hear more.

But Jacob continued. "War's gone on two years, boys. Ever hear 'em say, 'It'll be over by Christmas, surely!' Such a lie that is. Such a silly wish! Gonna go on and on, I suspect. And supply wagons gonna grow lighter and lighter 'til you can see the wood of their bed floors. Ain't never enough for all us. Not enough morphine. Not enough chloroform. Not enough bandages."

The following morning, after a sleepless night in our canvas tents, Corporal Jennings told us he'd just gotten word that the Confederates were on the move. The general had ordered a retreat. A nearby place called West Fort had fallen and even our reinforcements would be too late.

We were put back to marching, northward, up the same rutted and ragged road we'd come down the day before. There was bold talk up and down the line about needing just one last go at the Rebels to put them in their place once and for all. I joined in, boasting about my shooting ability and how I would pop a cork and celebrate in a manner of three weeks, for certainly now that Marshall and I were in the army, the Rebels would last no longer. Some soldiers laughed at my attitude, others cheered it. But in spite of my bravado, I kept thinking of Jacob and his missing foot. And then of Ethan Bowler with no legs at all. My own legs hurt for a moment, until I stomped around to get rid of the phantom pain. It will not happen to me, I know. I am too quick. I am too strong.

Just as the sun began to sink below the hills to the west, I heard a sound like nothing I ever imagined. It was far away, and had an uncanny echo through the trees, like the wail of a fierce and exotic animal. A corporal told me that was what they call a rebel yell. The Rebs do that to frighten their enemy as they advance.

It must work. I saw healthy men turn pale at the sound.

It is now nighttime and I'm writing by a single candle. We're in a thickly wooded area a ways off the road where we hope Johnny Reb won't be able to see us. We did not pitch our tents for we're not here long. Marshall and those not on watch have curled up on the ground for a few minutes rest.

Orders are that by midnight we will be moving north to try to escape the Confederate advance. They have a manner of maneuver where they form a long, crooked line like a fishhook to cut off a retreat. What a terrible thing, I must say, if I get captured without ever firing a shot or even seeing a boy in gray. Surely our fine commanders will not let us be cut off so. They will find a place for us to turn about and face our enemy to defeat him.

Even though we'll be heading back the way we came everybody seems in high spirits. There's nothing but talk of victory and even the wounded men being carried look like they want to rise up and keep fighting. I remember what Mr. Bowler said in town before we left. He said he was proud of his son, and I know he really was. It'd be something if somebody could say that about me someday.

I wish I could hear Uncle Silas' voice sometime. I'd like to hear him say that he really is proud of me. Ah, such a waste of a wish. It would never come to be.

I will try to write more later. It's getting late and it won't be long before we're on the move again.

11

"WE USED TO eat so fine back in New Jersey," said Simon as he rode in the wagon next to Susanne down Harrisburg Road toward Gettysburg. It was early afternoon, and the sun was hot enough to make Susanne want to throw her ridiculous kid gloves away, push up her sleeves, and take off her shoes. But Simon would tell, and she wasn't in the mood to have to defend her actions.

"Nothing like here," the boy said. "You would wish you'd been us! We lived in Trenton, and had a small garden ourselves, of course, but we had servants to tend the garden and cook our meals. But we would shop at the market as well, and get things no one could raise at home."

Susanne said, "Oh." She had her mind on other things. She'd not had a letter from Stephen since June 13, nearly two weeks ago, and she planned on stopping by the post office to see if another missive had arrived. As far as Susanne knew from the letter and the articles in the *Daily Gazette,* Stephen's outfit had not seen battle, but he and his fellow soldiers had been near it, or behind it, or in front of it. The letter had mentioned that they were heading north from Virginia, hopefully to engage the enemy in the border state of Maryland.

"Oh, we did," said Simon, nodding his head, causing his wide-brimmed hat to flop up and down over his pale face. "We ate shrimps and oysters, fresh from the sea. We had oranges from Florida. I've never seen an orange at your house."

"There's a war on," said Susanne.

A garter snake slithered across the road in front of Tim and vanished in a roadside growth of chicory and thistles, but Tim didn't so much as flick his huge ears.

"Yes, perhaps so," said Simon, not deterred. "We ate Underwood Deviled Ham and Van Camp's Pork and Beans by the cans full. I had all the Necco wafers I ever wanted for dessert. And sometimes just because I wanted them!"

Simon scratched his knuckles and babbled on and on about life and culinary delights in New Jersey. Susanne tried hard to tune out the burring of his voice.

Aunt Rudine had decided, with Uncle Silas' approval, that they should take in a hired boy to help work the farm. She had some money still and the investment, she felt, was well worth it. The corn was growing, as little as there was, but it was time to plant summer crops and Rudine still could not bring herself to allow Susanne, nor Simon, to do the heavy work of plowing. "Go into Gettsyburg," she'd said after breakfast this morning. "And post about these notices which I drew up last evening. One at the post office. Another at the courthouse, and perhaps the offices of the *Daily Gazette* and *Courier.* We shall offer food and lodging to a strong boy between twelve and fifteen, who is available and not involved in the local militia. A boy who is in good health and can remain with us at least through October."

Susanne took the notices. Uncle Silas insisted Simon accompany Susanne for a bit of fresh air.

When they reached the town, Simon was still rambling about his life in Trenton and the finery his family had enjoyed. "I'm sure we shall return when the war is done," he said. "I'm sure we needn't stay with you forever."

Susanne drew Tim up, right in the middle of the Diamond, causing other carts and wagon to steer around them. Several drivers called out that they should move to the side of the road. She looked Simon straight in the eye and said, "Tell me, do you want to be a child your entire life?"

Simon frowned.

"I asked you a question, and your mother would say you should respect your elders and not ignore what they ask."

"You aren't my elder."

"Oh but I am. By a few good years. Simon, I wish that you could hear yourself. I wish that you could see yourself. Are you truly happy whining, and complaining, and bragging? Do you ever wonder why no boys in Adams County have made you their friend?"

Simon sputtered, "That's mean!"

"No," said Susanne sternly. "It is not mean. Mean is if I were to shove you out of this wagon to the road and let the horses run over you, which I won't do, though I'm tempted. I'm stating truth. The Bible says the truth shall set you free. My father was a preacher, and I know it says that. Does it not bother your pride that we must take on a hired boy to do work you should be able to do yourself?"

"My mother says . . . ," stammered Simon.

"You are not ill. I do not see you roll about in a high fever. I see no rashes! You are spoiled rotten!"

"I am not!"

"I have watched you these past many weeks. You are not sick, you are pampered. You do not know what you can and cannot do for you never try! We could manage Sycamore Grove without a hired boy if you were to grow up just a bit!"

Simon drew his knees up to his chest. He put his chin down and closed his eyes for a moment. Then he looked at Susanne and said in a barely audible voice, "Mother said she can't take more losses in her life. She thinks me weak and is afraid for me to do most anything should I up and die. You see, Father didn't go off to war, he—"

"Out of the way this minute!"

The shout was directly in front of the wagon. A carriage loaded with passengers and luggage had come to a standstill. The driver was livid.

"Yes, sir!" said Susanne. She slapped the reins on Tim's back and steered him around the carriage. They ambled down Baltimore Street and pulled to the roadside in front of the *Courier*'s office. Susanne looked at Simon. "All right then, what were you saying about your father?"

Simon said, "Nothing."

"You said your father did not join the army."

"I said nothing!" cried Simon and he buried his face in his knees. "It is not your business!"

Susanne sighed. She shook her head. It was hopeless. He was who he was and had no desire to be otherwise.

The notices were posted about town with hammer and nail and the permission from the proprietors of the shops and offices on whose wall-sides the notices were hung. Simon remained sullenly silent the entire time, refusing even to get out of the wagon to hand nails to Susanne.

Susanne then drove the wagon to the post office, where she found no new letter from her brother. There was an old saying that no news was good news. She prayed this was the case. Then, outside, she waited for Tim to take a long drink from the roadside water trough. The heat of the day had become relentless.

Suddenly, a horse and rider came galloping down Baltimore Street. The rider was waving his arms madly, and shouting at the top of his lungs, something Susanne couldn't make out at first as he closed the distance between them. She remembered reading of Paul Revere in the Revolution, riding like the fires of hell were after him, warning the countryside of the advance of the British.

What is this . . . ?

"Rebels!" the man was screaming. "Militia, alert, muster quickly! Rebels on Chambersburg Street coming into town! Cavalry! Infantry! Militia, muster!"

Susanne's hand flew to her mouth. In the wagon, Simon squealed, "What? Rebels?"

The rider was by in a flash of hooves and dust, dodging wagons and others on horseback and on foot. Women and men on the street gasped and cried out. Several men from inside the post office slammed through the door to the walk, and asked Susanne, "Did we hear Rebels are on their way? Now?"

Susanne nodded. "Yes! Chambersburg Street!"

The men raced up Baltimore, swearing furiously. They were part of the town's militia, Susanne guessed, and were off for their weapons and to order their families into cellars and attics to hide from the danger.

From somewhere east of town came the sound of gunfire, rapid and loud.

"We've got to get out of town! We must get home!" Susanne shouted as she swung up into the seat beside Simon. She ripped her gloves from her hands and threw them to the road. She was much more capable without such trappings. She grabbed the reins, shouted "Yah!" then cracked the reins against Tim's hide with all her might.

Simon began to whimper. Susanne drove Tim east off Baltimore onto High Street, her feet planted securely against the floorboard. She shouted, "Stop crying! Perhaps it is a false alarm. We've had them before."

"But I hear guns!" came the small voice from beneath the wide-brimmed hat.

I do too, thought Susanne. *What else can it be but*

invaders? Her stomach twisted, and her fingers tightened even more around the leather reins.

They circled left onto Stratton, past homes and churches and barns. On this side street, citizens were just now catching wind of the warning. Shots grew louder, more intense, closer, echoing over rooftops and across churchyards. "What is it?" called a young woman who stood beneath a maple tree with several young children.

"Rebels!" called Susanne.

"Dear God!" cried the woman, and she and the children scattered like leaves.

Several boys in their early teens raced into the road, waving their weapons—pistols, shotguns, rifles—and shouting they would kill the gray-coated devils. "We'll send 'em back to hell where they came from!" one cried. Susanne had to draw Tim up short so as not to crash into the young militiamen, and wait until they were off the street and heading east toward the gunfire.

Simon clambered over the seat and dropped like a sack into the back of the wagon. He lay flat and covered his head with his hands.

At least he's not whining in my ear now!

The intersection of York was several blocks ahead. They would have to cross this road. The man who had warned the town of the imminent arrival of the enemy had said they were coming into town on Chambersburg, and York was the same road, just named differently on the eastern side of the Diamond. Surely, though, the militia—made up of loyal citizens and students from the Seminary, as well as a private boy's school—would be poised at the town square now, and would block any filthy rebels from going deeper into the town than the square. If Tim was quick enough, they would be out of the way before the Rebs could get this far.

The thundering gunfire escalated, with men yelling and cursing; clearly the militia and Rebs were exchanging rounds. *The Rebels shall never take our town!* Susanne thought. *The militia will not allow it!*

"Tim, extra oats tonight if you get us home!" She yanked the reins, maneuvering the wagon around a huge rut in the road and nearly missing a pig who squealed and scrambled beneath a road-side shed. Tim strained at his harness. It was clear the mule knew there was danger. The wagon shivered. In the back, Simon wailed.

"We're all right!" Susanne called.

They raced into the intersection.

And there was a deafening blast of gunfire to the left, very close, and a shout, "Halt, girl!"

For the briefest moment she thought of trying to get away, of screaming at Tim, "Run, boy!" but there was a line of rebels there, at least six of them, all pointing their rifles at her and at Simon and at Tim, and she knew that if they fired, one, or perhaps all of them, would be hit.

She drew back on the reins. Tim mewled and skidded to a halt. One rebel jumped forward and grabbed Tim's cheekstrap to hold him still. The mule shook his head but obeyed. Simon wailed, "We shall die!" and Susanne said, "Hush!"

With fury in her eyes and thunder in her chest, she said as calmly as she could, "Why did you stop us? We are not of the militia, nor have we any arms or food for you to steal."

Three of the rebels, with bristly beards and dust covered uniforms, burst out laughing. The others shook their heads. "A bold young woman we have here!" said one.

"She is indeed!" said another.

The rifles remained trained on Susanne and the wagon. Behind this cluster of Rebels, several blocks down York, Susanne could see Confederate soldiers swarming the Diamond, firing down streets and in the air. Others brandished swords as if they were flags. With dismay, Susanne could also see that many of the local militia had already been captured, and were being herded into the center of the square, their weapons stripped from them.

They took us by surprise, Susanne thought. *How could this happen? What is to become of us now?*

"God help us!" cried Simon.

"Oh, we don't mistake you for militia, missy," said one rebel, a boy of no more than seventeen with big eyes and brown teeth. "But what about that boy with you? I seen boys his age in town militias. What's wrong with him? Can't he fire a rifle? Or is he just simple-minded?"

Simon's eyes grew huge, and for the first time, Susanne saw a blaze of righteous indignation burn there. "I am not simple-minded!" he hissed.

"Then a coward," laughed one of the men. "We seen our share of both these past two years. Look at 'em fellows! A simple-minded coward!"

Another man said, "It's your nag we want. That mule."

"Tim?"

"He's got a name, has he?" said the Reb. "Sweet."

"Bet he tastes sweet," said another. "Better'n beef!"

It was all Susanne could do to keep from lunging at the man. For a blinding second, she remembered the fire in Rhode Island, when the house was ablaze and she and Stephen were returning from a Christmas party at another farm. It was evening and frosty cold, and the sound of the fire-bells was harsh on the air like discordant holiday music. The smell of smoke was acrid, thick, and as soon as Susanne saw the flames she jumped from the back of the hay wagon in which the children were riding and raced to the scene. Neighbors were there, a brigade formed from the river and well, passing buckets to the inferno, and Susanne ran up to the fire, close enough to singe her face, and reached out to pull away a blazing beam. She cried "Mother! Father!" and thrust her arms into the fire to find them but they weren't there. She was dragged away by strong, sympathizing men who said, "They're gone, dear, we're sorry, so sorry!"

So so sorry.

Susanne blinked, and gained control of herself at that moment so she would not lash out at the rebel, for surely she would be burned if she did. The men ordered Simon and Susanne out of the wagon, and then took the wagon and the mule back toward the Diamond, where the rebel bugle and drum corp had begun playing "Dixie." Women were crying out of attic windows, and elderly men who were not part of the militia stood about watching in horrified fascination. Several Gettysburg dogs were snarling and snapping at the intruders, who kept them at a distance with well-aimed kicks. More gunfire could be heard from off the square, and then several more clusters of militia were herded to join their fellows under guard.

"We are honored you have so welcomed us into your fine town!" cried one red-haired officer, who sat on his horse with his hat pushed back. "On behalf of our commander, General Jubal Early, we thank you for the gentle reception." He waved his hand in the direction of another mounted man, who nodded almost elegantly to the frightened crowd. He was slender and tall, though slouched in his saddle as if wearied of the ride. His gray beard was as wild and untended as forest brush. His gray-brown hat sported a long and shiny black feature. He lifted his hand to the townsfolk as if they had invited him there and he was the welcomed guest. "Now," continued the other officer, "we shall refresh our supplies. And we shall not steal. We are not the heathens you've heard tell about. We shall pay for what we need. With the money from our homeland, our country. The Confederate States of America. You shopkeepers shall honor our Confederate money, and show it and us the respect we deserve! What is this town, now? Gettysburg? Gettysburg sounds like a fine place to refresh our empty stomachs and our emptying haversacks."

There was more rifle-fire then, aimed in all directions—some biting the road not far from Susanne's feet—victorious blasts that caused the women in attics to withdraw and dogs on the road to slink away. Simon cried out at the new round of shots, and Susanne thought, *Coward he is! I am cursed with such a baby!*

Susanne took Simon by the arm sharply. She whispered, "Let us be out of here while their attention is elsewhere!"

"But—!" began Simon. Susanne grabbed his hand and turned from the terrible scene at the Diamond. They had to get home. They had to warn Uncle Silas and the aunts that the Rebels were in town. And rebels would surely be on the march again. They may even go up Harrisburg Road.

They ran.

With Simon wheezing and stumbling, they hurried up Stratton, past homes Susanne knew were filled with horrified women and children, hiding and praying for the Rebels to go away. They clambered over the railroad tracks and at last reached Harrisburg Road. The gunfire paused and then began again, perhaps more celebration at the siege of the town or perhaps more fighting. Susanne shouted, "We have to get off the road. They may come this way. We must go home through the fields!"

"I can't run back to the farm!" cried Simon. "It's three miles. I can't run three miles!"

Susanne squeezed the boy's hand until she knew it hurt. She didn't care. He had to understand! "You can and you will! If I must do this in a damnable hoop petticoat you can do it in trousers! You've no choice except run or let the Rebs have you! I don't doubt they will change their minds about capturing you and holding you prisoner with the militiamen. Now run!"

Simon ran. They crossed the uneven grassy stretch behind the Alms House and climbed the fence that separated its property from that of the closest farm. They forced their way northward through cornfields and woods, over streams and around ponds, past lazy cattle waving their tails against flies and sheep which ran at the sight of them. The sun beat down relentlessly, and Susanne had to wipe the sweat from her eyes with constant swipes of her hand.

Several times they stopped to catch their breath behind cedar thickets or large-trunked oaks. Simon clutched his sides as they rested, and then his legs, breathing as if he would explode. His eyes filled with tears, but he was no longer whining. No longer complaining.

At long last, the fields of Sycamore Grove were ahead. Susanne felt her energy rise when the familiar barn came in sight, and then the farmhouse with its privy and hen house and Dutch oven.

"We made it!" she gasped, then pushed ahead of Simon. She brushed through the gate and rushed up the path to the kitchen. Her skirt was soiled and the hem torn to ribbons. She would mend it later, as surely Aunt Rudine would point out the problem.

But not now. Not that there was danger.

Susanne slammed open the kitchen door and nearly fell into the room. Panting deeply, she grabbed the edge of the small table and called, "Uncle Silas! Uncle Silas, there's Rebs in Gettysburg!"

There was no answer from the parlor.

"Uncle Silas?"

No answer.

Susanne forced her wobbly legs to carry her into the parlor. Her uncle's bed was empty.

What has happened?

"Uncle Silas? Aunt Darcy?"

There was no human sound inside the house.

God! Have the Rebels sent a detachment up our road, and has my family been kidnapped or killed?

"Hello!" she cried, moving to the base of the stairs. "Please, someone answer!"

There was no sound. There were no voices. The

house was empty, and her heavy breathing echoed frighteningly loud.

"Susanne?" called Simon from the kitchen. Susanne left the hall for the parlor. They were gone. They had vanished. How would she explain this to Simon? What was she supposed to do? They could go looking for them, but what if Rebels were just down the lane now?

Sweet Jesus have mercy on us!

The boy was seated on his stool by the cook stove. His head was hanging down and he, too, was panting furiously. Susanne noticed his hat was long gone, fallen away in some neighbor's cattle pasture most likely, much like her own hat had been lost so many weeks ago on her last race with Stephen. The boy's face was sweaty, his light hair plastered to his head and the skin of his forehead and nose dreadfully burned by the sun. In his clenched fist was a note.

"See?" he asked through his teeth. "Was on the table."

Susanne shook her head and snatched the paper from him. It was written in Aunt Rudine's ladylike script, though hastily. It read simply, "Church."

"Church," said Susanne. "They've all gone to church? Uncle Silas? He can't walk! Aunt Darcy? She hasn't left this house in at least four years! What are they doing there?"

Simon shrugged.

It was then that Susanne saw the blood on his trouser leg. It had soaked through, from thigh to ankle.

"Simon!" Susanne cried.

"I'm not a coward and I'm not simple-minded," he whimpered. "That bloody Rebel called me a simple-minded coward, and I'm not!"

Susanne quickly took a carving knife and sliced the pants leg. A minié ball had grazed and split the flesh on his thigh just above the knee. The wound was not deep but could have been nothing but extremely painful.

Susanne knelt before Simon and touched it carefully. Simon flinched but did not cry.

"You were struck before we left town!"

Simon nodded.

"Why didn't you say something? I made you run clear from Gettysburg to the farm. Why didn't you show me your leg?"

"I'm not a coward."

"Simon . . . !"

"I'm *not* a coward!" said Simon.

Susanne sat back on her heels. She put her hands to her eyes and felt the pounding behind them. The muscles in her legs began to complain and tremble, in protest against the abuse they'd just taken. "Simon," she said softly. Then she said, "I see that now. You aren't a coward."

Simon shook his head.

"And no more a whiner, either?"

Simon shook his head. A tear rolled down his sun scorched face and he touched it with the heel of his hand.

Susanne took the boy in a hug, and he did not pull away.

Then at last she said, "We must bind your leg, then, and I will be off to the church. You stay here and hide in the cellar if you must. With God's help, I will find our family safe in His house."

"All right."

"All right, then."

Twenty minutes later, Susanne was back on the road, this time alone. Although her legs screamed in protest at being put to work again so soon after the recent abuse, she took the lane to Harrisburg Road, looked carefully before coming out of her hiding spot behind a tall weeping willow, then crossed over to a narrow path that led through the forest to St. Mark's Methodist Church.

The church was not far when taking the road, and

even shorter when cutting through the woods, but Susanne found her vision fading in and out as the heat of the day once again pressed down on her head and took her breath away.

"Let them be safe," she whispered as she untangled her foot from a vine of honeysuckle which had wrapped around her ankle and pushed ahead. "There has been too much to bear today. Let them be safe!"

The church was a simple wooden structure, planted in a clearing surrounded by pines. The yard around the church was dried mud, packed hard by the wagons and carriages and horses that brought worshippers on Sundays. There was a short steeple, a front stoop, and windows lining either side.

Susanne saw several horses and a single cart in the yard. *Should I recognize those horses?* she wondered, but her weary mind refused to cooperate. *Do I know the owners of those animals? Or are they renegades, who have stolen my family away to this church, and the note the brief cry for help from Aunt Rudine?*

Susanne crept to the first window. As slowly as she could, she leaned over to peer inside, clutching the scabby wooden planks that made up the walls of the church. She prayed that she would not be seen by whoever was inside.

That whatever was inside was not something she was afraid to see.

Clustered about the pot-bellied stove in the center of the sanctuary were Aunt Rudine, Mr. and Mrs. Olson and their two young daughters, and Mr. and Mrs. Anderson. Uncle Silas was on a pew, propped against the back with his legs stretched out on the seat, looking very worn and afraid.

There were no rebels to be seen.

Susanne burst through the front door. "I thought you were dead! I thought you were taken! What are you doing here?"

Mrs. Olson hurried to Susanne and eased her down

on a pew near her uncle. The wood of the pew smelled of soap and polish. Obviously Reverend Manning's wife had been in this morning, scrubbing and preparing the church for services the day after tomorrow.

"Susanne, are you all right?" asked Mrs. Olson. "Have you been running! Of course you have. My dear, you look simply exhausted. Are the rebel soldiers after you?"

"You've seen them?" gasped Susanne.

"Not seen them," said Mr. Olson. He was a short man with a receding hairline. "We heard they were in the area. Some boys were hunting in Pratt's Woods and they met a drifter who had seen encampments of gray uniforms near Cashtown. The boys went from farm to farm north of town, letting us know. And then Mr. Anderson came up from town, saying they were no longer in Cashtown, they were coming into Gettysburg!"

"It's true!" said Susanne. "I saw them!"

Aunt Rudine folded her hands in silent prayer. Uncle Silas swore under his breath. Mrs. Olson said, "We came to your farm as quickly as we could, and urged your family to come hide with us in the church until the danger passed."

"How hard is a church to find?" growled Uncle Silas. "Right off the road, we are. We aren't fooling anyone!"

"We agreed that the best place was God's house," said Mr. Anderson. "We agreed that if they were going to take our animals and our food, the Lord might forgive them. But if they saw fit to chase us out of God's temple to take hostages, then they would have more than the wrath of the Union Army to face, they would have the wrath of the Almighty Himself!"

"Amen!" said Mrs. Olson.

"Where is Simon?" asked Aunt Rudine, suddenly aware that Susanne had come alone.

"At the farmhouse," said Susanne. "Hiding in the cellar."

"Why didn't you bring him with you! Foolish girl,

have you no mind whatsoever? He won't know what to do!"

"He promised to stay out of sight until we return."

"He's not well! He's not strong!"

"He is stronger than you think, Aunt Rudine," Susanne said. Now wasn't the time to mention Simon's injury. It would do nothing but stir up emotions that were already buzzing like hornets in a nest.

"And look at you!" said Aunt Rudine. "Your hair!"

"My hair is not important right now, Aunt Rudine."

Then Susanne saw that the gathering wasn't complete. She looked around her, at the pews, at the altar, at the four corners of the room. "Where," she asked, "is Aunt Darcy?"

"Run off, that crazy old woman!" shouted Uncle Silas. "Got her as far as the door to the church and then she tore away from us and disappeared in the trees. Screaming that the spirit had her now that she was out of the house, that she was doomed, damned! Let her go, I say! Let her have her way and be done with it!"

"What?" cried Susanne, leaping to her feet.

Mrs. Olson took Susanne's hand and gave Uncle Silas a stern look that insisted he hush. She said gently, "Dear, we called for her. My own husband tried to stop her and bring her back, but she was gone, swallowed up in the trees. From even this far away we could hear commotion in town, shots as loud as cannon fire, and knew we had to stay put or risk all our lives."

"Without Aunt Darcy?"

"It sounds cruel, I know—"

"It does indeed sound cruel!" shouted Susanne. "She's an old lady. Her head is not clear! She will be frightened! She will get lost!"

"We had no choice," said Mr. Olson.

This is wrong, so wrong! Susanne thought. *This day is not real, it is a bad dream and I shall awaken soon and bless the morning sun and the sound of Uncle Silas coughing on his parlor bed. Yes, this must be a bad dream.*

And then, before God or anyone else could answer, she felt the world rush up to meet her, and she fainted.

12

"WE NEED RIDERS!" came the cry from far up the dusty, weed-choked road. Stephen was aching and hot from marching with his heavy haversack and weapon, and Marshall seemed to be feeling the strain as well, but at the call for horsemen, both of them perked up and strained to hear what the hubbub was about. It was midday, and their company had been marching northward through the rolling, thickly wooded Maryland countryside since dawn, having narrowly made their escape from Winchester, which the Rebels now controlled. Many of the remnants of General Robert Milroy's division had been captured during their retreat, and only by the grace of God had Stephen's company escaped unscathed. Until now, the only point of interest were the relentless gnats and mosquitoes that had taken a liking to Stephen's face and neck and the song some nameless recruit was singing up in the line.

"Mine eyes have seen the glory of the coming of the Lord,
He is stamping out the vintage where the grapes of wrath are stored.

He hath loosed the faithful lightning of His terrible swift sword."

And many of the men sang the following stanza with him, though many mumbled it as an afterthought. "His truth is marching on."

Far ahead, Stephen could see a pair of blue-uniformed, mounted horsemen, plodding slowly alongside the column of marching men. It was these cavalrymen who had been calling out, and both Stephen and Marshall were tempted to break from the ranks to answer them. To do so, however, would surely incur the wrath of their commanding officer—a fiery-tempered first Lieutenant named Carswell—so they both maintained their pace as patiently as they could. For simply asking where they were going, Marshall had been thoroughly tongue lashed by their CO, who was barely older than either of them but stood for no nonsense from anyone. So far, Stephen thought, they had scarcely encountered an officer or ranking enlisted man who *didn't* have an ornery disposition. And since leaving their camp, the thirty-two men of his company had been shuffled from one regiment to another, as if no one were quite sure what to do with them.

I would never expect such disarray in any army, Stephen thought, *much less in the army of the United States of America.* From all the chatter Stephen had heard around campfires and along the endless road, the Confederates were well-organized, with high morale, and superb officers. *No wonder the Rebels had made such advances.*

"Riders for the cavalry!" came the cry again. "Experienced riders only. Dangerous duty! Five extra dollars a month!"

The mounted men were drawing nearer, and now and again, someone would raise his hand and be pulled aside, presumably to be interviewed by the cavalrymen. Stephen saw that the horses the men rode were rugged, beautiful stallions, and the riders' uniforms were spotless, their leather boots polished, their spurs gleaming.

"We've gotta go for it," Marshall said, leaning over to Stephen. "This is our chance for some *real* excitement!"

Stephen nodded. Marshall was right. So far, they had marched themselves half to death, seen distant explosions, heard the screams of wounded men, and run through the darkness as if the devil was at their heels, but as yet, they had not so much as glimpsed an actual rebel. And now, at the sight of the horses, Stephen's mind went back to those carefree days of riding through the hills and valleys, of racing Susanne, of feeling like the master of the world. *Which was what I hoped the army would do for me*, he thought.

"Ho there!" he called, raising his hand as the cavalrymen came within acceptable earshot. Marshall's hand shot up as well. "We're riders!"

The nearest of the horsemen, a corporal, reined his mount toward them, giving both of them stern looks of appraisal. "What kind of horse am I riding, private?" he asked Stephen.

"A crossbreed it appears," Stephen replied confidently. "Likely a Thoroughbred and Arabian mix from the cup of the nose and the length of the legs. I reckon he stands about sixteen hands high."

The corporal's eyebrow raised as if impressed. He nodded. "How long have you been riding, son?"

"Since I was old enough to hold onto the reins. I'm only the best horseman in Adams County, Pennsylvania!"

The corporal appeared unimpressed. "What about you," he asked Marshall.

"Same's him," the blond boy answered. "We've grown up together and rode about every day."

"Step out of the line and wait over there," the corporal said, pointing to a tree where a couple of other young men had gathered in the shade of its low branches.

Stephen's heart leaped with excitement, and he clapped Marshall on the shoulder. They hurried off the road to the tree, grateful to get out of the sun's glare, if even for a short time. Stephen saw the corporal's partner conferring with Lt. Carswell, who seemed relatively sedate in the company of the cavalrymen. Stephen recognized the two men under the tree, but didn't know their names. He had seen them at various times during their march.

"Hello there," he said. "Going for the cavalry?"

"Yup," said one, a dark-haired man of about twenty-five. "I've wanted to be a horseman from the day I joined up."

"Same here," said the other, a short, lean fellow with auburn hair and bushy eyebrows. "It'd sure beat marching a footpath day in and day out."

"Damn right," Stephen chuckled in agreement, and was about to tell them about the fine horses he had back home when the corporal approached them and dismounted.

"Gentlemen, we're forming a new regiment for the United States cavalry. If you men have what it takes, you'll be out of the infantry and riding in the next few days. We're bracing for a major attack by the Rebels, and we need every available man for the job. Now, we're forming up at Five Forks. Corporal Sullivan there is going to make arrangements with your CO for the transfer. But if you wash out, you'll be right back in these infantry ranks again. Clear on that?"

"Very clear, corporal!" Stephen said, finally feeling that things were starting to take a turn for the better. *This could be the break I've been waiting for!*

When he saw Marshall grinning like a fox beneath his matted mustache, he knew his friend was feeling exactly the same as he. He ran his hand through the rough beard on his own sunburned face and suppressed a whoop of glee.

13

June 28, 1863

Aunt Darcy is not yet found!

My heart aches with not knowing where she is or how she is. God be with her and bring her home! She was never cruel to Stephen and me, yet we made sport of her behind her back. I am so sorry. Now, she may never return.

Mr. Olson and Mr. Anderson have looked for her but have yet to find her and she's been gone a full day and a half. They are down in the parlor, preparing to go again. I pray she is not dead!

I am banished to my room and my mattress, ashamed that I fainted like a child in the church right there in front of God and everyone. My mother never fainted. Yet down I went, cracking my head on the floor as I went. There is a gash along my crown, and someone—Mrs. Olson I suspect—has bandaged it up.

I am abed at the insistence of Aunt Rudine. I'm certain she has demanded I rest not out of love but because if harm comes to me she shall be saddled with more than her share of the chores about the farm.

I wish I could tack Molly and join the hunt for Aunt

Darcy, but Aunt Rudine will have none of it, and I must admit, at least to this paper, that I'm am light-headed and dizzy from my fall. From his bed, I can hear Uncle Silas complain to the other men that they should just let her be gone. How can he speak so of his wife? Has he never loved her, as my father loved my mother?

Ah, my head aches as if a cannon itself were firing inside. Such a ninny to faint!

Down the hall, Simon is recovering as well, with more of a reason to complain than I. But he is bound and determined to not make a sound. Aunt Rudine believes it is my fault her son is injured, and she dotes and wails about him as if he were at death's door. She believes his new stoicism is idiocy; that his injured leg has rendered him an imbecile! No matter how he tells her he will recover and that she needn't worry, she is certain the sun touched his brain and cooked and changed him. I admire the boy. I never would have thought I would say that. I wish Stephen could see him now.

The Rebels are gone from town, Mr. Olson has told us. Gone east from Gettysburg up York Road away from us all. They were in town but one day, yet only after having arrested 176 of the town militia, burning some of the train cars at the station, and stealing a good deal of food and provisions from town as well as farms on the western side of town when they arrived and those on the eastern side of town as they left. He says they will not be back. They've taken what they need and are gone for good. I'm sure he is right.

My head swirls. I feel as if I shall throw up.

Better now.

Beside my mattress is my set of paints and several of my paintings. The one I began of Aunt Darcy is between the mattress and the wall, and when Aunt Rudine is downstairs, I take it out to look at it. That lonely and frightened face at the kitchen window, watching out for her ghost. How much more afraid is she now? Tears come to my eyes. I miss her.

But she is gone.

And Stephen is gone.

Will they both return to us? Will I see either one again, and safe, and sound?

—Susanne Annalee Blackburn

14

MARSHALL AND STEPHEN looked each other over in their new uniforms, each admiring how much more distinguished they looked than in their old infantry garb. The clothes were well-fitted, white cotton muslin shirts; sky-blue trousers—the standard color for mounted enlisted men; belted, navy blue four-button sack coats; and heavy wool Kepi caps with the visors pulled low over their foreheads. But most impressive of all, Stephen thought, was the new firearm he'd been issued: a Sharps repeating rifle, which fired cartridge-encased bullets rather than minié balls, and did not need to be manually reloaded after each shot. It was much shorter and lighter than the Springfield he was used to carrying, so that it would be handy for firing from horseback. At his side hung a new, holstered .44 Colt revolver, as well as a sheathed, razor-sharp sabre.

Now he was beginning to feel like the soldier he truly wanted to be.

The training camp to which he and Marshall had been assigned—established on an extensive cattle farm in southern Maryland, much to the resentment of the property owners who clearly realized there was little they could do to chase the armed men away—was a sight to behold. It was filled with a great number of men, all of whom lived in tents, with a vast corral for horses beyond anything Stephen could ever have imagined. Where confusion had seemed the order of the day among the infantry, the cavalry appeared to be well-organized and professional. And the horses were magnificent.

Stephen had been tested on a beautiful, spirited Andalusian stallion, who seemed to take to him immediately. The muscular animal had a sleek brown coat and a chestnut-colored mane, and the moment Stephen stepped up to it and touched its muzzle, Stephen knew he'd made a new friend. Stephen had mounted the saddle with confidence and was told to take the horse through a course cut into the woods that surrounded the camp.

The horse, whose name was Rob but whom Stephen renamed Victory, seemed to know him better than any he had ever ridden, including his own beloved Fury back home. He had raced down the tight trail with ease, and leaped a broad creek as if it were a mere ditch. Stephen's spirit had soared with exhilaration, and he knew now that this life, indeed, was the calling of his heart. He had received top marks—even better than Marshall, who also performed well.

But then, he *knew* he would out-ride Marshall, he thought with a little smile to himself.

For three intense days, Stephen and the men of his new company practiced and drilled on horseback. The most challenging—even fearsome—drill was charging a number of straw dummies in the shape of human figures and slashing them with their swords. They were told that the cavalry often rode into battle in advance of the infantry and engaged the enemy in one-on-one combat. The riders were expected to be fearless and indefatigable; and they must be able to execute complicated maneuvers, the details of which could change in a moment during the heat of battle. Each man must be prepared to do his duty and never shrink from the fight into which he was ordered.

Stephen's arms were strong and agile, and he bore the sabre with ease. The first time his horse galloped down a short hill toward the first of the straw dummies, Stephen almost quailed, for he realized that, in actual combat, his blade would actually be meeting the flesh of another human being. But the orders of his instructors prevailed in his heart, and he brought the blade nimbly up and around, easily severing a straw limb from the scarecrow-like target.

With repeated practice, he was able to anticipate each of Victory's subtle moves, to learn at exactly what point he must begin the arc of his blade to deliver a killing blow. When he set his mind only to the task at hand, he found he was able to perform without fear or doubt.

Marshall seemed a little less sure of himself, though he rode his horse with almost the same expert technique as his best friend. When Marshall made his first pass at the scarecrow, he missed completely and fell from his mount, landing heavily upon the muddy ground, bruising his arm but wounding his pride more. The next time, however, determined not to humiliate himself again, he charged his target with a cry of determination, and neatly severed its "head."

Now, on the parade grounds near the entrance to the camp, Stephen and Marshall stood at attention with K Company, the unit to which they had been assigned. The other nine companies that comprised their regiment stood with them, awaiting the orders that would send them into battle, possibly into some strange region that neither Stephen nor Marshall had ever dreamed of before.

The regimental commander, a bushy-bearded colonel named Hawkins, stepped onto the platform before them and spoke in deep baritone voice. "Men, you are hereby officially commissioned as the 21st Pennsylvania Regiment of the United States Cavalry. You have all performed well, and I'm sure each of you will do credit to this great nation in battle.

"I've received orders that the 21st is to be incorporated into the 2nd Brigade of the 1st Cavalry division, which has been placed under the command of General John Buford. The 2nd Brigade is commanded by Colonel Thomas Devin, and consists of the 3rd West Virginia, the 6th and 9th New York, and the 17th Pennsylvania. You'll be in good company."

Stephen glanced at Marshall without turning his head. His friend was grinning broadly beneath his mustache. Stephen knew his own joy was not easily disguised, but at this moment, he didn't care.

"Now," continued Colonel Hawkins, placing his hands behind his back and tilting his chin upward. "I'm sure you're all anxious to receive your marching orders. Well, the Confederate Army has made tremendous advances under command of General Robert E. Lee. Word has come down from our new commander General George Meade that the Rebels are mounting a major invasion north from Virginia. The cavalry's been instrumental in slowing their progress, and we expect now to deal them a severe blow—one that will send them hollering back to where they came from!"

There was a cheer from some of the men behind Stephen, and Colonel Hawkins scowled. The men went silent. Hawkins then said, "We set out this very morning, gentlemen. We anticipate joining up with the 2nd Brigade three days from now. Our destination is Gettysburg."

Stephen's jaw fell. He could not help but look at his friend in dismay. Marshall's face had turned as ashen as the bleached wood of the platform upon which the Colonel stood.

"Good Christ," Stephen moaned softly. "After all of this, we're heading right back where we came from!"

15

"WE'VE GOT HER!" came the call from the back yard. It was Mr. Olson's voice, and Susanne, though still assigned to her bed by Aunt Rudine, got up on unsteady feet and hurried to the top of the stairs. Simon joined her from his room, hobbling through his door on the crutch Mr. Olson had made him from a whittled oak branch.

The kitchen door slammed open, and footsteps shuffled heavily into the parlor. Uncle Silas said, "Oh, so there you are! Where on God's green earth did you go, you old biddy?"

Then Mr. Anderson said, "Let's be kind, Mr. Preston, she's not well. Mrs. Preston, sit here on this chair. We need water, please!"

Aunt Rudine said, "Yes, of course."

Uncle Silas mumbled something Susanne couldn't hear.

"I'm going down," said Susanne.

"But you are in your nightdress!" said Simon.

"Nightdress be damned! I want to see how she is!"

"And leave me all alone up here?" Simon whined.

Susanne frowned at him, and he rolled his lips in

between his teeth. "I thought I'd heard the last of that tone," she said harshly. "Come down, too, if you'd like. That's what the crutch is for. Or not. Your choice."

"But Mother will . . . ," Simon stopped himself. Looking sheepish, he said, "I'm coming, too."

Downstairs in the parlor was a flurry of hushed activity. Aunt Rudine held a cup of water to Aunt Darcy's lips, but the old woman was refusing to drink. Mr. Anderson and Mr. Olson, having done their manly duties in finding the woman, weren't sure what they were supposed to do next, and stood at a distance with their arms crossed, hats crushed in their hands, and their dirt-crusted faces stony with concern.

"Aunt Darcy!" said Susanne. She moved to the old woman and gave her a hug. Though her head had begun to complain with the sudden movements, Susanne knew that her ache was nothing compared to the misery of the old woman. Darcy's face was scratched and bruised as were her arms. Her hair had been torn out in hunks, leaving bleeding bald patches of scalp. But her eyes were the worst. They were wide and staring, as if she'd seen into the very pit of hell.

"Susanne, your nightdress!" said Aunt Rudine.

"I'm covered, Aunt Rudine," said Susanne.

"Seems as if the war is hurting us even though we've not even held a rifle nor worn a uniform," said Mr. Olson. "Three in one family harmed because Rebels passed through Adams County."

Uncle Silas, his legs drawn up in bed to give his wife room to sit, said, "Pah!" and looked at the wall.

Aunt Rudine was worn out. Even her chastisement lacked its usual fervor. "Susanne, Simon, go back upstairs. We don't need you wearing yourself down with worry. We've too much grief in this house as it is."

"Not yet, please," said Susanne. Aunt Rudine's eyes narrowed with the challenge.

Mr. Olson and Mr. Anderson excused themselves

then, bowing and bidding the family farewell, then leaving quickly by the front door.

Susanne held her ground. She touched Aunt Darcy's hand, and slowly stood. The old woman's eyes suddenly focused, and her gaze caught Susanne's own. Susanne squeezed the hand gently, encouragingly.

Then the old woman whispered hoarsely, "I saw her."

"Saw whom?" asked Aunt Rudine.

"Pah!" said Uncle Silas. "Here she goes with the bloody ghost again! Alms House is where she belongs! Why didn't Mr. Olson and Mr. Anderson do us all a favor and take her there? Why do we have to suffer her flights of fancy?"

"Why do we have to suffer your constant complaints, Uncle Silas?" Susanne said suddenly. *Oh, mercy, I've said it, and now I'm sent away!* she thought. But there was no calling the words back. They were out. "Cruel words, as if her hearing is gone with her mind! She is frightened, Uncle Silas!"

"Susanne!" gasped Aunt Rudine. "How dare you speak so?"

"Why is it what we don't say so much more important than what we say?" Susanne pressed. *Sent away and gone. God help me. But the door is opened, not easily shut.* "Why is it proper to keep silent when what is said might help?"

"Impertinent!" gasped Aunt Rudine. She lifted her hand to strike Susanne's cheek, but Simon spoke up.

"Mother don't, Susanne is right."

"Simon, hush! You aren't yourself! Go upstairs now!"

"Aunt Rudine," said Susanne. "Would you prefer that if another rebel unit came up Harrisburg Road that we not know about it? Would not knowing make them go away, or would it save us from their attack?"

Aunt Darcy's head drooped, but her hand remained in Susanne's. Uncle Silas said, "Blasted abolitionist! If

I'd known her sentiments back then I'd never have married her!"

"Susanne, upstairs now," said Aunt Rudine. "You and Simon, this moment, or I shall strike you. Don't think I would not. Neither of you are thinking clearly, or you would not dare speak to me in such a manner!"

"If the house were on fire," Susanne continued, "would you not want to know as it is unpleasant news?" She swallowed, and in her mouth she could taste the years'-old flavor of soot and ash, and in the back of her mind she could see the flames of her Rhode Island house, licking the sky like a devil's hound. "Can there be anything so dangerous that it cannot be talked about, Aunt Rudine?"

"Was that slave woman," said Uncle Silas. He turned back over on his side to face the gathering in the parlor. "That slave woman your aunt tried to rescue five years ago."

"I saw her," muttered Aunt Darcy. "In Pratt's Woods. She chased me there, to the tree . . ." The words faded as if the old woman were falling away inside herself.

"What, Aunt Darcy?" asked Susanne. "What tree?"

"You think we should give up secrets, eh, Susanne?" said Uncle Silas. "You think knowing will make things better?"

Aunt Rudine took Susanne's arm but Susanne shook it off. Aunt Rudine sputtered with shock at the disobedience.

"Aunt Darcy, tell me," said Susanne. "It will make you feel better. It will help us all, knowing what has had you so dreadfully frightened all this time."

The old woman said nothing.

"She never wanted anyone to know," said Uncle Silas. "But I'll tell you if you want to know. Been wanting to tell for years but she begged me not to. But it can't make anything worse, can it?"

Susanne felt her blood chill at the impending story. She continued to hold her aunt's dry hand.

"Five years ago a runaway negress came up across our field and hid in the barn. Darcy, being the strong woman she once was, had her chores there, feeding the chickens and pigs, mucking out the stalls for the horses and the ox. She was a fine, strong woman, she was. Rudine, you remember."

Aunt Rudine nodded. Her arms were drawn around her waist. Clearly she did not wish to hear what her father had to say.

"The young wench was there in the stall, hiding in a corner. But Darcy took pity on her. Nitwit! Better had she beat the runaway with a shovel and called the authorities. But she didn't. She brought that young thing inside the house . . . my house . . . and gave her food and drink. I wouldn't stand for it, and I told them both so. Darcy said it was her house and she'd do as she pleased."

Susanne looked down at her aunt. She'd never know the woman to be anything but confused and helpless. It was hard picturing her as vibrant and out-spoken.

"I told her no woman would ever tell me what to do. I called for the authorities myself. It's a law that slaves can be taken back from northern states to their masters, who paid good cash money for them. And I take exception to anyone who says states have to bow to the government in Washington, D.C., who have, by the words of our great and evil president, declared all slaves to be free! Sick as I was I pulled myself from my bed and walked down the lane to the road where I stopped passers-by to help me."

"Father, don't upset yourself," said Aunt Rudine. "We don't need to hear this. Shh, please, now."

He ignored her, and rose in his bed like a phantom from the mire. His face was red with anger, years of anger, kept pent up inside. "Well, a fine bunch of volunteer slave catchers they turned out to be. Reward, they were hoping for. Whatever. I didn't care, long as she was gone! The girl ran off. I rode with the hunt, sick but determined, and we cornered her in Pratt's Woods under a tall oak. Darcy followed us, thinking she could change our minds."

"And she didn't," whispered Susanne.

"Blacks are dim-witted and this one was no different," said Uncle Silas. "Saw us closing in and she fashioned a noose with some wild grape vines. Climbed up into the branches of an oak. Secured the vine and slipped her head inside the noose. She pointed a finger at Darcy and then jumped from the branch. Her neck snapped like a chicken. Fool! Death instead of life? What kind of choice was that? We owned slaves when I was young. We fed them, clothed them, saw they had preaching of the Lord and a roof over their heads. This girl was like the lot of them, though, thinking there should be more. Selfish, silly darkies!"

"Whatever you say, Father," said Rudine. "Hush now, that's of the past."

"Your aunt," said Uncle Silas, training his gaze directly on Susanne, "has ever since believed the wench cursed her for allowing her to be caught. She has been afraid to leave this house for fear the ghost will destroy her."

"Aunt Darcy," said Susanne, turning the woman's face up to her own. But Aunt Darcy would not open her eyes. "It's all over. You have been outside, but you are not harmed, any more than some vines which tripped you and briars which cut you. There was no ghost. Only your secret."

"You can say it all you want," hissed Uncle Silas. "Lord knows I've tried. She won't hear it. She won't believe it."

"Perhaps," said Susanne. "But we have to try."

There was a long moment while no one spoke. The only sound was Uncle Silas' coughing and the nervous tapping of Aunt Rudine's toe on the wooden floor.

Then Susanne said, "She needs rest. Aunt Rudine, could we help her upstairs. Please?"

The old woman was ushered upstairs and put to bed. She said nothing more, but struggled with the bedcovers and then drifted into a fitful sleep.

Aunt Rudine grabbed Susanne by the shoulder in the hallway. Her face was a snarl. "As you seem well enough to come downstairs to take your great-aunt's side against my father and then help bring her upstairs, I dare say you are well enough to be out of that night-dress and back to some worthwhile occupation. There is a basket full of laundry to wash, and we've not had fresh eggs since you carelessly fell and hit your head. Off with you now."

Susanne went.

16

July 1, 1863

I must here confess that I am excited and terrified beyond anything I've ever known before. The sky is just starting to get light, the birds complaining to each other in shrill morning voices, but I haven't been able to sleep for hours. My regiment arrived at Gettysburg yesterday and we are now bivouacked east of Seminary Ridge. We thought we would meet up with more of our soldiers and move on in to find the Rebels and stop them in their northern advance. But we have learned that Rebels are not far from here, just up the road. And they are heading our way.

The time has come. I shall see battle at long last. Even though most of the men are still asleep, you can feel something in the air, like the air just before lightning strikes. As I sit on the damp ground not far from the Seminary where my father was trained for the ministry, I wonder how he would feel if he had looked out one of those windows to know one day men would prepare for battle on their holy ground? To know his son was one of them?

We met the rest of the 1st Brigade yesterday, near

Fairfield. The Brigade commander is a man named Gamble, who is gruff and has a voice like cannon fire. I think he is a smart man, in spite of his tendency to bellow. He led us on our march in advance of the rest of the 1st Division. We moved at a good pace on our horses, and it seemed so strange to be heading into such familiar territory. It was an exciting feeling, for our division numbers almost 3,000 men, and here we all came, riding proudly on our mounts.

We got into Gettysburg at about 11:30 yesterday morning, and it looked like everyone in town came out to watch our arrival. There were people on every street corner, yelling and cheering, and as we came riding down Washington Street, a bunch of women started singing "Our Union Forever." They didn't know all the words, but they kept singing the chorus over and over as if it was their gift to us. I saw old Mr. Bowler, who was waving and hollering, though I don't think he saw me, or if he did, he didn't recognize me. His son was there, too, sitting in a wheelchair, and he was cheering just as strong as anyone. I saw the Spilman sisters and then Jennie Wade, right next to them. She recognized me in my uniform, and waved lightly, and smiled. I sat up taller in my saddle and looked at her straight-on so she could truly see the man I have become. I half-hoped I'd see Susanne out to greet us, but knew the chance was slim.

Yet I don't know how I feel about being back here. I look forward to battle, yet wonder if I've not brought a curse on my family for bringing the battle here to Gettysburg.

It was here in Gettysburg where I got to see our division general, John Buford. He is a strong-looking, brown-haired man with a huge mustache and cleft chin. He rode on his horse, which he called Gray Eagle, smoking on his pipe and chatting cheerfully with all the people who wanted to talk to him. I heard someone say to him that a few companies of rebels came through town a few days before, ransacking stores and homes, which scared the people half to death. It was no wonder they were so happy to see us, because they feel like they are safe now.

I took to liking General Buford right away. He presents himself like the kind of man who could stand in the path of a bullet and it would never hit him. I can tell he is a brave fighting man, and I am sure he will lead us well. I think he is part of the reason there's this energy in the air this morning. Everyone knows the fight could be fierce and some of us won't see the sun come up tomorrow.

Gen. Buford sent a group of us—Marshall and me among them—to the north of town on the Bendersville Road this afternoon to scout the ridges, where there might be Confederate infantry. There are so many roads coming into town, the Rebels might choose any of them to make an advance. Col. Hawkins led our company through the woods to the west of the road, and we went up to Oak Hill where we could get a good view from high ground. It was an eerie feeling, for if I looked west, I could see about where our farm would be, obscured by the dense forest of Pratt's Woods. It's hard to imagine that the place I'd called home for four years could become a battlefield. Marshall made a joke about being able to go home for lunch in the middle of a row. I know he was teasing, for the laugh afterwards was forced. I pray any fighting will be well away from Sycamore Grove. I don't want anything to happen to my family. Family. I suppose they are, at that.

We never saw any rebels, but Col. Hawkins said he could smell them. We rode back into town late in the afternoon. The general has set up a pair of headquarters, one at the Blue Eagle Hotel, right in the middle of town, and another in the field out between the Mummasburg and Hagerstown Roads. Our brigade is camped a little farther north, near the Harrisburg Road. Near home. From what some other scouts said, we know that the main Confederate forces will be coming from the west. Gen. Buford has set up a number of picket positions at each of the main ridges in their path. This way, as the Rebels advance, they'll be slowed down at each ridge, and when the pickets retreat, they'll reinforce the post behind them.

Each of our brigades has a number of smaller groups posted around the main perimeters. These are called skirmishers. They're kind of like an early warning for us, so we won't be caught by surprise.

The sun is almost up and the men are starting to stir. It's surprisingly cool out this morning, and I'd almost like to stay wrapped in my bedroll, but my heart is pumping loudly already.

Oh, God. A shot! Another one! Something's happening, and close! I'll write later when I know what's going on!

If I get the chance!

17

July 1, 1863

It is but noonday, and we can hear it from the back-yard, rolling clear like summer thunder across the tree-tops and corn field.

Cannon fire. Gunfire, echoing north from Gettysburg. We can see the rise of gray smoke, and know a battle has ensued.

Mr. Olson rode over just a half-hour ago to see if we had heard the commotion. His family is fleeing north to Harrisburg to stay with relatives. Who knows, he said, in what direction the battle may turn? But we shall stay. Uncle Silas wants to stay, for he says Rebels would never hurt a compatriot. Aunt Darcy is still in her state, and has no thoughts to share on the matter. Simon, especially, wants to stay. He's told his mother she should let him have a rifle and let him go to town to join the fray. Of course, she forbade it. I don't know how I feel about it all.

We were certain the Rebels were gone for good when they left on the 27. We were certain that fate would not bring them back our way. But certainty is a foolish con-

cept, I'm learning, an idea swept away as easily as a leaf on the waters of Rock Creek.

I only pray the battle is quick and done with in a day. I can only thank God that Stephen is in Maryland.

—Susanne Annalee Blackburn

18

A PALE MIST crept over the fields and hillsides in an eerie morning calm. Just after dawn, Stephen and the men of the 26th had moved forward from their encampment to an area near the summit of Seminary Ridge, facing west, in the shadow of the Lutheran Seminary. The towering cupola of the structure provided a strategic view of what would surely be battlefield in the next few hours. Now dismounted with their horses tethered behind trees, the cavalrymen knelt with their rifles behind shrubs, large rocks, and barricades of fallen timber—any cover that the sloping terrain offered. From this point, Stephen could look down at the valley and the ridges rising beyond: McPherson Ridge, Herr Ridge, and Schoolhouse Ridge, all shrouded in a thin cotton-like fog. He knew that the Confederate Army was out there somewhere.

A deep rumble in the distance suddenly broke the silence.

"Listen," whispered Marshall, who was crouched by Stephen behind a gnarled cherry tree.

Enemy cannon fire. Stephen nodded.

Stephen's Regiment was the rearmost of Col. Gamble's 1st brigade, the rest of which was spread over East McPherson Ridge, to the west. To Stephen's right, stretching all the way over North Seminary Ridge, north of the Chambersburg Pike, the regiments of Col. Tom Devin's 2nd Cavalry Brigade had also dismounted and formed a defensive line, waiting—as they all waited—for the inevitable approach of the rebel army from the west. According to various sketchy reports passed up and down the line of men, the nearest threat was a large force of both infantry and artillery under command of Confederate General Henry Heth, now somewhere on the other side of Herr Ridge. Heth's division seemed to be pushing eastward with amazing confidence and efficiency—as if they were unaware of the massive resistance that awaited them just into the hills.

Earlier this morning, Stephen had heard a number of shots, and the men of his regiment had been told that some of Heth's advance skirmishers had run into Gamble's pickets and quickly retreated. A short but fierce fight ensued with muskets and cannon over on Schoolhouse Ridge, some miles away from where Stephen and fellow soldiers now waited with pounding hearts and sweating palms.

Marshall hummed a few notes of "Union Forever," then went silent when Stephen shook his head. Nearby, several of the horses whinnied and stamped their feet restlessly as, in the distance, the deep boom of cannon fire intensified. Vibrations pounded the earth as if Satan were hammering the ground, intent on splitting it asunder.

"Think they'll be shooting at us soon?" Marshall said softly.

"They're still a long way off," Stephen said. "Our cannons'll be on them before they can get anywhere near us."

A moment later, a loud *boom* rent the air, and a pillar of smoke rose slowly from the wooded crest of West McPherson Ridge, just half a mile away. Several more concussions rattled the earth, and more plumes of smoke rolled out of the swaying trees.

"That's theirs," Marshall said tightly. "That's their cannon fire."

Stephen heard a renewed neighing of horses, and turning, he saw General John Buford atop Gray Eagle, trotting toward the Seminary building several dozen yards to the rear. Stephen's heart leaped, and he hoped the general would look his way, just so he could see that gleam of pride for his men that seemed to always sparkle in the general's eyes.

"He's going from position to position, making sure everything is just as it should be," said Sgt. Mansfield, K Company's leader, who was kneeling behind a granite slab on Stephen's left. Mansfield was a tall, dark-haired man of thirty with huge, mutton-chop whiskers that covered most of his face. "Buford won't leave anything to chance," he said.

Stephen saw their stoic-looking, moustached brigade commander, Col. William Gamble, and the ruddy-faced leader of the 2nd brigade, Col. Tom Devin, galloping up to Buford's side. The two of them fell in next to him, and Stephen heard Gamble say, "I've put several hundred men up to bolster the skirmishers along Herr Ridge and Willoughby Run, sir. But they're having a hard time holding. Heth's got artillery over there, and it's playing hell."

"He's just now figuring out he's not up against the town militia," Col. Devin said. "If he figures he's got a big infantry force waiting for him, he'll slow down and play it more cautiously."

"He's a righteous appreciation for the tenacity of a well-equipped infantry," Buford said. "But he's going to take that high ground. There's no way around that now."

"We need Reynolds' 1st Infantry Corps in here now," Gamble said. "They're still several miles away, near's we can tell."

"We've got about an hour," Gen. Buford said, gazing past Stephen and Marshall toward the ridges in the west, his eyes narrowing beneath the brim of his hat. "Heth's got at least a brigade on either side of the pike." He pointed to the ribbon of the Chambersburg Pike that snaked off to the right near the base of Herr Ridge. "Reynolds *has* to get here."

As the officers rode away, Stephen swallowed hard. He knew the general had been talking about a life-or-death situation for all of them. If the reinforcements didn't arrive soon . . .

We could all die here, right on this hillside.

Time passed slowly as Stephen and Marshall watched and waited, smacking mosquitoes and gnats, frustrated that they could not see what was going on across the distance at Herr Ridge. Suddenly, musket fire erupted a short distance down the slope, amid a thick copse of trees. Stephen saw several puffs of white smoke, and he could now hear the cries of men from down in the valley.

A loud blast split the air, followed by another, then another. There was a sudden, shrill whistle, like a banshee, and a pillar of fire erupted from the earth several hundred yards to his left.

"Incoming fire!" cried one of his fellows to the right.

Stephen raised his rifle, peering desperately down the hillside, his pulse slamming through his ears so loudly it drowned out the distant thunder of cannons. Marshall glanced at him, no longer looking like a sharp, confident soldier, but a frightened lad who wished to be anywhere but here.

Stephen felt the ground shake beneath him, and at first he thought a number of cannons must have discharged nearby; then he realized the thunder came from the hoofs of several horses. Turning, he saw a uniformed officer with long, dark brown hair riding up on a sleek black horse, accompanied by several escorting riders. Gen. Buford suddenly appeared at the upper window of the seminary building, a shine of relief softening the chiseled features of his face. "What's the matter, John?" cried the officer on horseback.

"The devil's to pay!" called out Buford. "General Reynolds, your services are much needed."

Stephen saw his commander disappear from the window, only to reappear at the seminary door a few moments later, adjusting his gloves and his hat. General John Reynolds rode forward to meet him.

"My corps is three miles out of town and coming double-quick," Reynolds said. "I hope you can hold out a while longer."

Stephen's heart leaped at the sight of Buford's steady gaze into the distance, the confident jutting of his chin. "I reckon I can," Buford said without emotion. "The firing line is right over there," he said, pointing toward Herr Ridge. "Gamble's pickets are getting hit hard."

Gen. Reynolds nodded thoughtfully. Buford called for his horse to be brought up by one of the corporals, and a moment later, he was again mounted on Gray Eagle. As Stephen watched, the two officers raced quickly away, to the north, off to inspect the battle line. As another volley of cannon fire sent columns of smoke into the air a few hundred yards away, Stephen suddenly found himself wondering why he had at one time so looked forward to facing off against his rebel adversary.

"26th Pennsylvania!" called a familiar voice off to Stephen's right. He saw the stout figure of Col. Hawkins approaching on horseback. "Everyone move to the left. Everyone to the left. They're coming in on the flank of the 8th New York. Everyone to the left!"

Stephen scrambled to his feet and joined the rush to the horses as men began to move from their positions. His blood now ran cold, for if there was anything about tactics he remembered from his training, it was that a regiment being attacked from the flank was going to suffer heavy casualties. Stephen hurried toward his mount with Marshall close on his heels.

Victory snorted as Stephen, with shaking hands, untied the reins from the tree branch. "Hold boy, hold," he whispered, realizing that the words he spoke were as much for himself as for his animal. He slammed his boot into the stirrup and swung into the saddle, then gathered the reins and coaxed Victory in place. The ranks formed with Col. Hawkins in the lead. Sgt. Mansfield held up his hand, signaling K Company to wait for the other companies to line up and then fall in behind them. As the regiment began to move, Stephen and Marshall took their places and reined their mounts to a brisk trot.

"Here we come, Johnny Reb," Marshall called out, his bravado betrayed by a cracking voice. Stephen saw his friend's fingers fiercely clutching his carbine in one hand, his eyes darting nervously back and forth. Marshall knew as well as he that, as they moved southward, they were drawing nearer to their brigade's deteriorating line—and the enemy—and farther from the rest of their own securely entrenched comrades.

The regiment rode quickly down a slope and then up another, skirting the Fairfield Road, which stretched away to the south and west. Stephen had ridden this same route on Fury numerous times before, but now, the whole countryside seemed unrecognizable. Great and stinking clots of smoke drifted like filthy clouds overhead. For a moment, Stephen thought he heard the distant sound of men screaming.

Victory seemed oblivious to the atmosphere of strangeness on this July morning. These horses had been bred and raised for just this kind of duty and proceeded as stoically as any seasoned military man. Stephen suddenly wished he hadn't named his horse. He remembered being told that it didn't pay to have friends in combat for you could lose them. And as Fury had been his friend, Victory had become one, too.

He loosened several fingers from the reins and strummed them on the animal's warm, sleek shoulder. Victory seemed to notice the attention, and shook his head proudly.

Not far ahead, Stephen saw a line of blue-coated figures crouched along a wooden fence, rifles raised and firing intermittently into a hollow amid the encroaching trees at the base of McPherson Ridge. The air was drenched in a thick, acrid haze of gunpowder smoke. And down in that hollow, Stephen caught his first glimpse of his gray-coated adversaries.

A seemingly impossible number of them.

"Oh, my God!" he whispered to himself. There seemed to be no end to the lines of rebel soldiers massed several hundred yards down the slope. Stephen could see that, beyond the enemy infantry, up on the crest of Herr Ridge, a row of cannons had been placed to clear the way for their advance. The crackle of gunfire was constant and growing louder every second. Then, the cannons roared, their muzzles spewing flames and smoke. And off to the right, a series of explosions racked the earth as the cannon shot struck.

Col. Hawkins now turned, leading the regiment to the left of the wooden fence, lifting his sabre and pointing out the direction for the men to guide their horses. Sgt. Mansfield rode up beside Stephen, pointing to the blue-uniformed cavalrymen crouching near the fence. "That's the 8th New York," he said. "End of Col. Gamble's line."

"We're a long way from the rest of our brigade," Marshall shouted. "A long way!"

"We go where we're needed," Mansfield said. "We're the United States Cavalry!"

They pushed on another few minutes along the edge of a dense cluster of evergreens and oaks. Then Col. Hawkins drew to a halt and called, "Dismount! Tie your mounts! Take positions to the left! To the left! Go! Go!"

Stephen dropped from the saddle, and secured Victory to the nearest tree. He gave his stallion a reassuring pat on the muzzle, and then joined the other men as they ran after the sergeant toward the edge of the hill.

Suddenly, he heard a whizzing sound, followed shortly by another, then another. And before his eyes, one of the men of his company let out a gasp of shock, spun around to face Stephen, and then fell heavily to the ground. In that moment, Stephen saw that a deep, black hole had opened in the man's forehead, unleashing a flow of thick red blood. The man's limbs twitched for a moment, then he lay still.

"Sweet Jesus!" Stephen whispered.

"Move, boy, move!" cried the man behind him, shoving him forward before he could be trampled by the rush of men. He picked up his feet and ran as fast as he could, clutching his rifle so tightly his knuckles hurt. He glanced around, looking for Marshall, but he could no longer see his friend.

Another round of whizzing sounds burned in his ears, and, nearby, a pair of men fell, one of them screaming shrilly as he clutched his shoulder. Stephen saw that the man's arm flopped and dangled uselessly, and white bone showed through a vicious-looking rip in his skin. Nearby, the deafening thunder of rifles discharging simultaneously pierced Stephen's eardrums, and a thick veil of white smoke suddenly obscured the line of Confederates far down the hill.

There was a pair of tall poplars to Stephen's left, and he stumbled toward them, unable to hear anything but a shrill ringing in his ears. Trying to remember his training—to stay calm and not panic—he knelt beside the tree, lifted his rifle and fingered a bullet on his ammunition belt. Then he took a deep, steadying breath, as a number of men from his company took positions near him, attempting to wedge themselves as near to the trees as possible for cover.

He saw Sgt. Mansfield step up a few feet away, peering into the cloud of smoke, sword still drawn. He looked around at the company to determine their positions relative to the enemy, then nodded as if satisfied with their vantage point. He lifted his sword and called out, "K company! Load weapons!" Around him, Stephen heard the sharp *snap-click* of numerous carbines being cocked. He slipped his bullet into the breech and pulled the bolt home. "Ready!" came the command. Stephen lifted his rifle and aimed it into the slowly thinning cloud of smoke. Now, he could see the Confederates—many of them now shockingly close as they advanced up the hill. "Aim!" cried Sgt. Mansfield. Stephen lowered his head and sighted down the barrel with his right eye, as he'd been trained. He saw a number of men in firing range. Heart pounding like a cannon, he selected a target.

"Fire!"

Stephen sucked in a breath and squeezed the trigger. The Sharps rifle bucked in his hands and the roar of the shot stung his ears. A plume of smoke obscured his vision for a moment . . . but when it cleared, he saw the man he'd aimed at staggering drunkenly, a huge patch of red spreading over his left shoulder. The man then fell, out of Stephen's sight.

"Oh, no," he whispered, his lower lip quivering. "Oh, what have I done?"

"Reload and fire at will!" Sgt. Mansfield called. Stephen knew that with his breech-loading carbine, he could get off four or five shots to the enemy's one. He loaded and cocked his rifle again and aimed at the still-advancing graycoats, swallowing hard, silently telling himself that if he didn't do his duty, he was going to die on this hill.

Suddenly, he realized that a number of Confederate men were moving around to the left, going for the company's flank. Spurred by the terrifying thought of being overrun, he swiveled his body, calling out, "To the left! To the left!" Sgt. Mansfield glanced over, recognized the approaching threat, and swished the air with his sword, directing a number of the men to change the direction of their fire.

Stephen drew a bead on the nearest of the enemy men—about fifty yards down the hill. Again, he squeezed the trigger and the gun kicked. But this time when the smoke cleared, Stephen saw he had missed. And now, above the thunder and cracking of gunfire, he heard a chilling, shrill cry from down the hill. The sheer volume told him that an unbelievable number of men must be beginning a charge. He quickly reloaded, took aim again, and fired.

The man in his sights dropped to the ground and out of view.

The gunfire from below was louder now. And then, he heard a loud *thwack,* very close to his head. Glancing around, he saw a splintered hole in the tree where a minié ball had struck. It was close.

God, so close!

A series of rifle shots sounded all around him, and the enemy that had been advancing to the left suddenly seemed to disappear. A few stragglers began moving back to the right, and Stephen aimed at one of them, getting off a shot that took the man down like a felled tree.

A hand suddenly clapped Stephen on the shoulder, and he looked around to see Sgt. Mansfield nodding grimly at him. "Good work, boy," he said. "You just earned your dollar."

"Thank you, sergeant," he whispered hoarsely, taking the moment's respite to draw a deep breath and steady his nerves. The advance was far from over; at best he had only a few seconds before he was in the thick of it again. And even before he could reload his rifle, another volley of shots came from below, and another minié ball smacked the tree near him, a few inches higher than the first.

There was a commotion behind Stephen. A man on horseback came galloping from the north, hunched low to present as small a target as possible. He called out to Col. Hawkins, who had taken a position a short distance to Stephen's right, "Col. Hawkins! Sir! Your regiment is to pull back and reinforce the 8th New York's right flank!"

"Who's that order from?" Hawkins growled.

"Straight from Col. Gamble, sir!" The man's horse bucked and wheeled around as bullets zoomed through the air on all sides. "Oh, Col. Hawkins—Gen. Reynolds has been killed. A little while ago."

"Damn!" Hawkins cried. "All right, then . . . company commanders! Get your men mounted up and ride back to the right! Double-quick!"

Stephen rose, only to see a huge mass of gray-clad figures rushing up the hill directly below, only a hundred yards away and moving fast. Unable to stifle the cry of panic that came from his lips, he turned and sprinted back toward the edge of the trees where the company had left its horses. He prayed that Victory had not been hit by a stray bullet or injured in any way. Now, thanking his heavenly Father, he saw the familiar, saddled horses standing near the trees as if waiting patiently for their masters, each of them looking as calm as if the nearest enemy bullet were miles and miles away.

But the threat, Stephen knew, was much nearer than that. As if to emphasize the thought, the crack of musket fire sounded close behind, and he heard the frightening *whizzing* of minié balls through the air, horribly close to his head. He found Victory amid the other horses, slipped the knot in the reins and leaped into the saddle. Stephen drove his heels into the horse's sides and Victory leaped forward, almost throwing him right back off. Stephen gripped the reins fiercely with one hand while holding his carbine in the other, hoping he might be able to fire off a parting shot the moment the wave of rebels crested the hill.

And then, another terrible cry split the air, a raw,

shrill noise that barely sounded human—the dreadful "rebel yell." He saw a number of Confederate men appear near the position he had just vacated, their muskets aimed at the retreating cavalry. As one, they fired, and he saw several men fall from their mounts. One of them, a young man whose name was Kendrick—who Stephen had learned was only fifteen years old—was just about to reach his horse when the back of his head seemed to simply cave in. The boy's eyes blew out. Crimson blood splashed over his neck and shoulders, and he fell into the grass without a sound, only a dozen yards from Stephen.

They're moving to the right. They're going to cut me off!

It was true. The Rebels were scurrying like demons over the top of the hill, guns firing, bayonets flashing. Stephen saw a few more of his companions fall from their horses, and now he knew he could not possibly follow those who had already begun their retreat without being cut down. He looked desperately around for any sign of Marshall, but he had no idea where he might find his friend—or even if he were still alive. The one thing he knew was that he must move, and move quickly.

He saw a number of rebels rushing in his direction, muskets raised; again the shrill, terrifying rebel yell split the air, drowning out even the sound of gunfire. Gripping the reins with his right hand, he lifted the carbine in his left and fired. The bullet found its mark in a rebel's chest, and the man fell, only to be replaced by three more coming over the top of the hill.

Stephen had no time to reload. He hung the rifle over his shoulder by its sling and drew his heavy sabre from its sheath. He knew he had to retreat to the left, but men in gray coats were starting to pour over the crest in that direction, too.

This is it, he thought. *I break free or die trying.*

His entire body clenched against the fear, he raised

his sword and charged, crying out at the top of his lungs, praying his fury would put enough terror into the hearts of the Rebels to scatter them—just long enough for him to dash away into the trees ahead. He saw at least four men directly in front of him. One of them raised his musket, its muzzle aiming straight at Stephen's chest. Without thinking, his reflexes taking over, he swung his sabre, barely clinging to the rushing horse. He felt the blade meet something that yielded stubbornly to its force, and he heard a horrible scream of agony and disbelief. Something warm and wet splashed his hand, and when he glanced back, he saw the rebel soldier had fallen to the ground, rolling and crying in a shrill voice.

The man's arm lay by his body, gushing scarlet blood.

Tears burned in Stephen's eyes as he rode ahead like the devil, now only yards from the safety of the thick woods, where rebel bullets wouldn't likely find him. He heard several cracks of gunfire, and the terrible *hum* of a minié ball passing close to his ear. Suddenly, his horse lurched, screeching in pain, and Stephen saw blood spurting from the side of the horse's neck, just below its mane. The horse staggered, bellowed, then bucked. Stephen lost his grip on the reins. His sabre fell from his hand, and he found himself tumbling on the hard ground. The horse crashed to the ground near him, kicked once, then lay still.

"Oh, God," he groaned, trying to pick himself up. "God!"

With a loud *smack,* a bullet struck the horse in the flank, spraying Stephen with more blood. But the animal did not so much as shudder. It was dead.

Stephen's rifle had slipped from his shoulder, and his sword lay somewhere beyond his sight. He could still hear the shouts of the Rebels and the continuous crack of gunfire, but for the moment, no bullets seemed to be hurtling his way. He saw his rifle a few feet away, crawled toward it and snatched it up, then, with a groan, he rose to his shaking feet and began running for the cover of the nearest tree, some ten feet ahead.

Once under cover the low branches, he dropped to his knees and sucked in one painful breath after another. He had been jarred from his fall, and he knew he'd be bruised, but nothing seemed to be broken. He'd taken worse tumbles when riding Fury. But he was alone here, and at least a regiment of enemy infantry now stood between him and his own company—whatever might be left of it. He had seen numerous men falling in the withering fire, and wondered how many might have reached safety. What about Marshall? What could have happened to his best friend?

After a few moments, the reality of what he'd just experienced began to settle heavily upon him. How many men had he shot? Three? Four? And—to his horror—he could still see the bloody, severed arm of the man he'd attacked with his sword. The rebel's screams had been full of pain and disbelief. He could scarcely imagine what it must be like to lose a limb in such violent manner. But he'd *had* to do it. If he hadn't struck first, the soldier would have shot him dead. If Stephen hadn't ruined the man's body, he might have taken Stephen's life.

That is what this war is about, he thought. *You have to be the first to kill or you're going to die.*

His breathing began to steady, and he knew he would have to be moving on. He was hardly safe here. The Rebels would surely be scouring the woods, the fields, any place that might hide an enemy. He rose wearily to his feet and began running deeper into the trees, heading in what he thought was a southeasterly direction. The ground sloped gradually downward before rising again, and he knew he was near the southwestern edge of Seminary Ridge. To his right lay Fairfield Road, which could lead him back into Gettysburg. But he also knew that the Confederates would be swarming that way, and the chances of finding safety there were not good. If he pushed on eastward, he would come to Cemetery Hill, and there, he thought, lay his best chance of hooking up with a friendly unit.

He didn't know what time it was, but the sun had passed the noonday mark at least an hour ago. With every step he took, the gunfire behind him grew more distant, and finally he began to feel that the immediate threat was past.

But his relief was short-lived. As he stumbled on through the cover of the trees, he heard the heavy tramp of feet somewhere to his left. He could hear voices as well, and the call of an officer directing his men to skirt the edge of the woods—right where he was hiding. He didn't know whether the troops were Union or Confederate. He feared that an advance regiment of the troops that had wiped out his company might have made it this far east if they'd pressed hard in their charge. If they found him, he had only two choices: surrender, and end up in some filthy rebel prison camp; or stand his ground and take out as many as he could before they shot him dead.

To live in disgrace, or to die with honor?

I want to live.

What had he thought when he joined? That this war was going to be a fine adventure, where everyone who played would get to go home after it was over and tell heroic stories around the fireplace to their enthralled families?

I've had enough. I've seen enough! I want to go home.

He heard footsteps coming nearer and saw shadows moving at the edge of the trees, a hundred feet or so to his left. He cautiously pulled a bullet from his ammunition belt and slipped the round into the chamber of his carbine and cocked it. Then he slipped his .44 Colt from its holster, made sure the ball was seated, and pulled back the hammer. With rifle in one hand and pistol in the other, he braced himself against the bole of a tree, facing the oncoming infantry, realizing that he had just made his decision.

What he didn't expect was to be suddenly grabbed from behind and pulled from his feet. His weapons fell to the ground, and a great weight fell atop him. He scrabbled desperately at his attacker with his fingernails, but the strong grip on his shoulders did not relent.

"Hold it!" called a voice. "Stokes, he's one of ours!"

The stout body rolled off of him, and Stephen found himself looking into four pairs of eyes beneath dirty blue kepi caps. He saw the red, white, and blue insignia of the Union Army. And breathed a sigh of heartfelt relief.

"Good Christ, I might've shot everyone of you!" Stephen exclaimed breathlessly.

His remark was met with a round of mirthful chuckles. "You're lucky Stokes didn't just cut your throat right then," one man said. The husky fellow named Stokes winked at him, then picked up Stephen's weapons and handed them back to him. "He's a habit o' doing that to strangers. You all right? You got blood on you."

Stephen looked down at himself. He had been splashed by the blood of both the man he'd maimed and his own horse. "I'm all right," he said softly. "It's not mine."

"You're a cavalryman," another one said. "What unit you with?"

"26th Pennsylvania. We got tore up in a charge just a little while ago."

"You're out of luck," Stokes said. "I don't think there's a living horse between here and Mummasburg Road. At least, not on our side."

"We're with the 159th Pennsylvania Infantry, Company C," the first man said. "I reckon you'll want to come along with us. You try to find your regiment again, you're going to be cut down. There's nothing but gray as far as you can see over that way." He pointed to the west.

"Which way you going?"

Stokes pointed to the south and east. "On our way to shore up the lines way down the Taneytown Road. A hill called Little Round Top, so I hear."

Stephen nodded, just happy to have been found by a friendly outfit. "I'm with you," he said. "I'll try to regroup with my unit whenever this is over."

"Come along then," one of the men said. "Got no time to waste,'cause the devil's on our heels."

Stephen holstered his Colt and shouldered his rifle, following the men toward the edge of the field and the rest of the regiment that was marching quickly to the south and east. He realized he was hungry and thirsty, but all his gear was on his dead horse. He'd just have to make do, he thought. *At least, for now, I'm still alive.*

He could only hope that Marshall was too.

It may not pay to have friends. But I do have one, and dear God in heaven, I don't want to lose him!

19

THE EVENING FELL with a startling silence to the south of Sycamore Grove, and Susanne knew the fighting was done.

But was it over?

She knew nothing of warfare, save what her brother had told her when reading from the *Daily Gazette*. Men determined to have their own way, determined to kill for what they wanted or just so others would leave them alone.

Stephen went to war to be left alone, to get away from those who plagued him at home.

The day had been spent in tense, uneasy normality. Susanne, now back with the active members of the household, emptied bedpans for both Uncle Silas and Aunt Darcy, collected eggs, fed Molly and gave her a cube of sugar she'd smuggled from the kitchen, mended torn sheets, and baked venison pie in the Dutch oven. Simon hobbled about on his crutch, saying very little, whittling a stick on his stool and reading from some of the novels his mother had brought with her from New Jersey.

Every so often there was an unusually loud explosion

from the south, and Susanne would flinch and her stomach would tighten, but then she put her mind back to the task at hand.

By twilight, supper was over and everyone was settled down to their routine—Rudine tatting in her parlor chair, the slender silver hook moving steadily and easily about the tiny white threads, weaving the center of a delicate rose doily. Her face relaxed at this task, the lines of irritability softening and her mouth losing its terse and proper frown. Uncle Silas was propped in his bed reading his Bible, his lips moving silently as he took in the Word of the Lord. Simon sat at the parlor table, working at the arithmetic problems Aunt Rudine had assigned him. Lanterns placed about the room and candles lit in sconces on the wall allowed everyone enough light to proceed with their particular activity.

Susanne was across from Simon with her watercolor paints. Aunt Rudine had told her to try her hand at copying a painting in a book she'd brought from New Jersey, a pastoral landscape with sheep and a flute-playing shepherd on a hillside. But she found her paint brush wavering, not wanting to make a sheep, but wanting to paint what she saw at that moment.

She looked at Aunt Rudine, and began to move the color on the paper, and in a few minutes, a simple but lovely image of her aunt was preserved, in a rare and peaceful moment.

"Susanne!" Aunt Rudine looked up from her tatting. "That doesn't look like the picture I told you to copy! What is that you've done? Show me!"

"Nothing," said Susanne, running her brush through the details of eyes and nose and cheek, bleeding the colors into a muddy patch that could, with some effort, become a hillside for sheep and their shepherd. "I'm trying. I shall get it right."

After creating a semblance of a landscape with white spaces left for where the sheep would be, Susanne excused herself and went upstairs to check on Aunt Darcy.

The woman had not spoken since the day before, though lay with her eyes closed as if in a trance. Susanne sneaked her paint brush and a few wells of paint with her and, having collected the half-finished portrait from between the wall and her mattress in the sewing room, sat by her ailing aunt's bedside.

"Aunt Darcy?" Susanne whispered, touching the woman's shoulder. "Can you hear me?"

The woman stirred but did not open her eyes.

Susanne placed the paint wells on the window sill, and began to work on the picture in her lap. She finished the yard first, adding the daisies that lined the path and the black-eyed Susans that pressed their sturdy stems and orange blossoms against the side of the house. Then she finished the shutters on the kitchen window with a dash of brown, and last, the countenance of her aunt, gazing into the distance.

"It seems we find what we look for, don't we, Aunt Darcy?" Susanne said softly as she painted, putting the blue to the eyes, the pink to the lips. "My father used to preach that from his pulpit, though I never thought about it before. He would say, 'My dear brethren, we have been born with two sets of eyes. One set is the eyes of God. The other, the eyes of the devil. Which eyes do you use to observe your world, my friends? Which do you use to contemplate your neighbors and your fellow man?' He was right, Aunt Darcy. You watched for your ghost as penance, and you saw her. Stephen and I looked for the irritable in you, and found that, I'm sorry to say. I looked for the brat in Simon, and oh! It was right there in front of my eyes. But it seems now that there may be goodness that we miss because of own stubborn minds. That is sad, isn't it?"

"Susanne?" called Aunt Rudine from the base of the stairs. "How long must you be up there? She can't hear you. She doesn't know you're with her. You've got painting to do, and I see nothing on your paper but smudges and smears!"

Susanne could barely suppress a grin. "Certainly there is beauty we miss, Aunt Darcy, but sometimes. . . ."

"Susanne!"

"Coming, Aunt Rudine!" Susanne gave her great-aunt a quick kiss to the cheek, returned the painting to her room, and started down the steps with the brush and paints.

Half-way down, there was a knock on the door. Susanne flew the rest of the way and yanked the door open. Sticky summer night air wafted in around the man on the stoop.

"Mr. Anderson, do come in!" said Susanne. "Are you well? Is your family safe?"

"Oh, certainly," Mr. Anderson said with a quick nod. He stepped into the hallway. He pulled his hat from his head and twirled it anxiously in his hands. "They are fine. We are all fine, thank you. There was no fighting near us, nor near Sycamore Grove. I rode out to the site of the battle as close as I could, and spoke briefly with several of the scouts. It seems the armies are still around and in town. The Rebels have chased our boys out of Gettysburg and have taken up residence in some of the homes and stores. Others are scattered about the west and southwest, holding our boys at a disadvantage on Cemetery Hill and other knolls. We've suffered terrible losses. But our men are poised to fight again tomorrow."

"Oh," said Simon, who had limped to the parlor door. "How dreadful!"

"Yes," said Mr. Anderson. "Dreadful is the word. If only the Rebels weren't so stubborn. If only they had not been so hell-bent to have their own country and rip ours apart! Pardon my language, ma'am."

"Oh, stop the rhetoric, Daniel!" called Uncle Silas form the parlor. The commotion had awakened him. "I think they are right to fight! Those are my friends in gray out there, you know!"

Aunt Rudine came up behind Simon and put her hand

on top of his head. "Thank you for the report, Mr. Anderson. It is kind of you to let us know what has transpired, and that our farm seems to be out of the realm of danger."

"Well, ma'am," said Mr. Anderson. "The main reason I came was to let you know about Stephen. He's here. He's fighting with the cavalry in Gettysburg."

Susanne grabbed for the wall. "He is here? That's impossible! The last I heard he was in Maryland!"

"Soldiers go where they are told to go, Miss," said Mr. Anderson. "He was seen riding through town the afternoon of the 30."

"Impossible!"

"No, I'm afraid it is quite possible. Mr. Bowler saw him on the street with the other cavalrymen. He and his son and wife escaped their home when the fighting started across Seminary Ridge. Lord, who knows what will be left of Gettysburg when this is done? Rebels might burn his tannery, will likely steal everything that isn't nailed down."

"They were lucky to have gotten out without being shot!" said Simon.

"Yes," said Mr. Anderson. "They came to our farm and are staying with us until the fighting's over. Mr. Bowler told me he'd seen Stephen. I thought you'd want to know."

Susanne's chest constricted. Her scarred arms broke out in a rash of sweat. "We have to do something," she said.

Mr. Anderson shook his head. "Miss, there is nothing we can do but sit tight, pray, and protect what is ours."

"But Stephen *is* ours!"

"Don't upset yourself," said Aunt Rudine. "I don't want you swooning again."

"I just stopped by to let you know," said Mr. Anderson. "A peaceful evening to you all. We shall say our prayers for Stephen tonight."

"Good night," muttered Susanne. Mr. Anderson left,

and Susanne dropped down on the bottom step.

"You'll soil your dress, child," said Aunt Rudine.

"I want to go to Gettysburg and find Stephen," said Susanne.

"What? You'll do no such thing."

"Aunt Rudine, I've tried my best to be the lady you think I should be. Oh, how I have tried! But it is never good enough, never quite right. Before you came, I didn't get into trouble, I didn't act a ruffian, though you would believe otherwise! Perhaps I didn't put my hair in a snood, perhaps I'd never played a flute, but I did much, and what I did was right and good."

Aunt Rudine stomped her foot. "Hush this minute, child!"

"I am going to find Stephen, to see if he is safe. I shall be careful. I shall ride quietly. I know the land around Gettysburg as well as anyone, for Stephen and I used to race our horses all over. I shall go to find him, for I shall not be able to rest another moment if I do not know his fate!"

Aunt Rudine's face twitched with fury. Uncle Silas said, "I need to sleep! Would you ladies please be silent?" Simon glanced from his mother to his cousin and chewed on his lip.

Then Rudine said, "Very well, then. You have certainly made your point. What use have I to argue? Go find your brother if you can. But do me one small favor? Would you please wear your bonnet and some gloves? Should anyone we know see you, I would wither to think they thought I'd let you out of the house improperly."

Susanne let out a long breath, and stood on the step. "Of course, Aunt Rudine. I can do at least that." She turned and trotted up the steps and into her room. The bonnet was on the back of the sewing chair. Her gloves had been thrown to the street in town a few days ago, but perhaps Aunt Rudine would lend her . . .

The sewing room door slammed shut. Susanne spun

around. She could hear the key turning in the lock.

"What are you doing?" cried Susanne.

"You shall not go to town!" cried Aunt Rudine from the hall. "I won't lose you, do you hear me? You go to town, they capture you, kidnap you and shoot you! I will not let anyone else get lost, young lady! I will not allow it! You may cry all you like but this door stays locked until you come to your senses!"

Susanne threw herself against the solid wood. "Aunt Rudine, please!"

But she could hear the footsteps back up the hall, then down the stairs. Susanne rattled the knob and slammed her shoulder on the door, but it did not give. It was a door Stephen had repaired in March. "Curses on you, Stephen, you do things too well!"

She slammed the door one last time and slowly went to the window and stared out. Her fingers strummed furious patterns in the dust on the sill. *Lose me, indeed! She doesn't own me! What is wrong with that woman, that she is so angry, so cruel, so selfish!*

The yard outside was filled with shadows and moonlight. Clothes on the line hung heavy and motionless. An owl in a distant tree called balefully, and a fox barked for its mate.

Aunt Rudine's muted voice drifted from the open parlor window, rambling on about the bandage-rolling party she would have next week, since the first one she'd hostessed had been such a success, and how surely Darcy would be better by then. Surely she would be out of her silly state and back on her feet.

The yard was not that far below. Susanne studied the ground. The grass was dead and dry, but long and thick. If she jumped, the worst that could happen would be that she would break an ankle or a leg.

But I've fallen from Molly before and come up unscathed. I know how to fall without being hurt.

She snatched up her journal and pencil and stuck them into the deep pocket in her skirt. She didn't know what she might find, or who might—God forbid—find her. This way, she could send a letter or leave a note if worse came to worse.

Pushing the glass up farther and swinging her leg over the sill, Susanne offered one quick prayer, "Lord do not let me get hurt before I can find out what's happened to Stephen!" and pushed herself off. Warm summer air rushed past her ears and her skirt flew up over her face, but before she could even wonder what Aunt Rudine would think of such impropriety, she struck the ground and immediately buckled her knees so she would roll, unharmed, in the brittle grass. She clawed her skirt away from her face and lay for a moment, staring up at the stars and the moon and the branches of the trees that laced themselves like black skeleton's fingers over the sky.

And then she was up, bolting around the side of the house to the backyard, racing down the path to the barn, where she yanked off her hoop petticoat and tossed it into Fury's empty stall. She tacked Molly, led her out of the barn, and swung into the saddle. "We've got business in town," she whispered in her mare's ear. And with a shrill clucking and a slap of the reins, the two took off across the cornfield in the pale light of the July moon, hoofs and hearts pounding wildly.

20

July 2, 1863

My life has been changed. I could never have imagined in a thousand years—a million!—that I could live through a day like yesterday. It's around two in the morning, and I haven't been able to catch more than a few winks of sleep all night long. I am lucky to be alive, though I wonder if I will ever get to write in this journal again. I was fortunate enough to find a regiment that pulled far enough back from the front line during the night to enjoy a good fire and some fresh vegetables and chicken donated by a nearby farm, and some preaching from a company chaplain who didn't just stand up before us and talk about fighting for the glory of God, he got down with us by the fire and said—with tears in his eyes—he knew God wept for the wounded and for the dead.

Within two hours we'll be on the move again. We're camped just off Taneytown Road, and I expect we will arrive at Little Round Top well before noon. It's a Pennsylvania regiment, the 156th, but there's men from all over joined up here. It's a part of General Hancock's II Corps, I hear, but I don't even know who the brigade or division commanders are, or even if those officers are still alive. Everyone is tired and there are lots of walking, wounded men. What a horrible thing to see: men wrapped in bloody bandages, some with mangled limbs or missing an eye, but still moving as if death has just refused to take them.

I have no idea where Marshall is. My hand trembles as I write the words. Such a fine friend! He always made me laugh, he could always cheer me when I was angry or upset. Yet he may well be dead. I saw so many of my regiment get killed in the battle yesterday, and now that I can look back on it, I feel guilty to be alive. I understand so well why I was told not to have friends in combat. But I did. I took that chance. I asked the chaplain to pray for Marshall when he sat at the fire with us. He smiled at me and said, "I will, son. But it might come better from you."

I have prayed. But I can't tell if my prayer is answered or not. Is Marshall dead? Is he alive? Is he lying half-dead in a field, part of himself blown away? The thoughts are like razors, flaying me alive inside.

Somebody told me that at the end of the fighting yesterday, the remaining cavalry units were moved away from the front to rest after all of the terrible fighting. I may never get back to my regiment, if there's anything left of it. I know K Company was pretty much wiped out. I saw Sgt. Mansfield dead on the field. I saw Col. Hawkins lying on the ground, I don't know if he was dead or not.

I know I killed several men and cut off a rebel's arm. Two days ago I would think I'd be proud of what I have done, but now I feel sick to my stomach at the thought of it. I know it was my duty, and if I didn't kill I might have died. But they were just men, and boys, and I was close enough to see their eyes and their pain. Some of those wounded men were screaming for their mamas before they died and I've never heard anything so sorrowful in my life. I never want to hear it again. It's so hard even to write now. I've tears in my eyes and they keep coming, down my cheeks to my chin, and my sleeves are soaked with wiping them away. I know I've got to be a man, but they won't stop.

I wonder what's happened to Uncle Silas, Aunt Darcy, Aunt Rudine, Simon, and especially Susanne. I don't know how far north the battle may have reached. Were they near the fighting? Were they hurt? If I only had thought of them when I left home. Vexations they were to me, but what is vexation to blood and death? I wanted to be a man, and I suppose I've become one, but what kind of man am I? I helped bring this bloody war home, right to my very door. I have killed other men. I may die myself. God only knows.

One of the boys tonight at the fire, a lad named Douglas, said he had a brother in the Confederate Army. Said his brother went to school in North Carolina, and decided that it was right that the Confederates should have their own country. Douglas said he wrote his brother when the war broke out two years ago and said to come home to Philadelphia. But his brother was fired up and sure the Rebs were right. Now, Douglas says, his brother is captured, a prisoner of war at Camp Douglas, Illinois, an irony of names that didn't make any of the soldiers seated near him laugh, including me. Another boy said his cousin, an infantryman from Vermont, was imprisoned at a Confederate camp called Andersonville. I asked what the place was like. He said he didn't know, but hoped it wasn't too bad.

I wonder if there had been some other way to resolve our differences. I thought fighting would be exciting. Oh, Marshall and I thought it would be so fine! Yet I'd never seen a man lying on the cold earth screaming for his family before. A man with intestines pouring from the wound that had been his gut. Now I have. Now I can't help but wonder. People have been fighting forever, I know, and nothing changes no matter what. How come we're not better than the people who lived a hun-

dred years ago, or a thousand? Can't we learn from the men who die before us?

Somehow I feel like one of the men who nailed Jesus to the cross. Weren't they just doing their duty?

I can't write any more. It'd be nice to get a little sleep before the bugle blows.

21

July 2, 1863

It is near dawn. I have made it into Gettysburg, after tethering Molly to a tree behind the Alms House. Some of the inmates were howling inside, and lanterns are burning in nearly every room. I don't doubt they've been terrified all day, with the fighting so close to them. I shouldn't be surprised if they are all tied to their beds tonight to keep them from harming their keepers.

There are some Confederate patrols in the streets of Gettysburg. They are the same color as the streets, coated in dust from toe to head, and blend in like some moths blend in with the bark of trees. I've had to tread lightly in the shadows so as not to be caught by surprise.

And oh! The sounds that echo up and down the streets and alleys! If I were to die and find myself at hell's door, I cannot imagine I would hear sounds any more pitiful. It seems as if the very churches and homes themselves are in agony, and the very bricks and mortar are crying. There must be many men in those places, brought up from the battlegrounds to be tended with their injuries.

They all sound like Stephen. How will I find him? Will I find him?

I am seated now in an alley, under the scratchy branches of a boxwood hedge. The only light by which I write is the moonlight and some faint pooling of lantern light from the garret of a nearby house. After I catch my breath and my courage, I shall move to one of the town's many churches. There, I will be safe from capture, for I still believe that even filthy Rebels respect the house of God.

There I shall begin my search in earnest.

—Susanne Annalee Blackburn

22

LITTLE ROUND TOP was a domed hill with steep, rocky sides, which had been largely cleared of timber in previous years. Its taller brother, Big Round Top, lay a short distance to the south, already a strategic lookout post for the battered but still potent rebel enemy. The advance of the southernmost elements of the Confederate army, largely made up of Alabama men, meant that Little Round Top was the last major barrier between them and the besieged town of Gettysburg.

Stephen had found himself linked up with a disciplined, relatively fit unit, well-armed and high-spirited. Many of the men of the 159th Pennsylvania were combat-hardened veterans of previous battles, and were considered one of the most honored regiments in General Meade's Army. Stephen had been given fresh water and some food, and had slept under a comfortable blanket. His body ached from having toppled from his poor horse, but at least he wasn't otherwise wounded.

The Union lines had been strengthened to the west of the southward-leading Taneytown Road, along the edges of a large wheat field and, southeast of that, a broad peach orchard. But the 159th marched past those lines on their way to Little Round Top, which, for the present, was defended only by a small number of men from the Union Signal Corps. There had been much shooting just beyond the peach orchard, but Stephen and the Pennsylvania regiment did not pause to engage. Instead, they marched double-quick toward the rising hills ahead, knowing that if the Rebels took over Little Round Top, their victory was almost a certainty.

Stephen had briefly seen the regimental commander, a chiseled-faced colonel with mutton-chop whiskers and long copper-colored hair named Tourneur. Some of the men in Stephen's new company said that, though he'd been born in the United States, his French blood was strong, and he still spoke with a pronounced French accent. The Colonel constantly called, "Vite! Vite!" as the men marched, urging them to hurry the pace.

C Company's sergeant was a short-haired Philadelphia man named Craighill, who seemed genuinely pleased to have Stephen join up, even temporarily. "We need every hand that can hold a gun," he told Stephen. "Hope you'll get back to your unit, but we'll take you as long as we can keep you."

To Stephen's relief, the regiment stayed mostly away from the field of fire for the better part of the day, though he knew they would probably be in the thick of it again sometime before dark. And sure enough, well into the afternoon, Stephen saw a large number of blue-coated men moving double-quick on their left flank, heading in the same direction as his regiment. Shortly, a rider came along and called to Col. Tourneur, "Sir, we're from Col. Vincent's 3rd Brigade. We've got the 20th Maine, the 44th New York and the 83rd Pennsylvania. The Rebs are routing the lines toward Little Round Top. We've got to make a stand!"

Tourneur nodded and said, "We will join you. Men . . . vite!"

Stephen saw the boulder-strewn side of the hill ahead, and realized that they would have to climb as fast as they could. If they were overtaken by the rebel forces, they could be picked off the sides of the hill like apples from a tree. On the other hand, if they gained the high ground, and the Rebels were forced to make an upward assault, every advantage would be theirs.

Except for numbers, he thought. *They're still going to outnumber us!*

Stephen pulled in several deep breaths to fortify his muscles, and followed Sgt. Craighill's men as they began the arduous climb. The craggy boulders were both a help and a hindrance; some of them provided natural hand- and footholds, but others acted as barriers that significantly slowed their progress. Every foot gained, Stephen felt better, yet still apprehensive. If rebel gunmen opened fire now, the exposed climbers were as good as dead. But all around him, men from four regiments were going up the hill at top speed. It was an impressive sight.

"Hall, Wandrey, and Vestoff!" Craighill called from just ahead of Stephen. He was pointing to a rocky outcropping that provided a natural bulwark against attack from below. "You three, take a position here! Parker, Scott, Millay . . . and you, Stokes . . . over there!" Stephen was pleased to see that the sergeant appeared to be a natural leader, a quick thinker on his feet, and assured in his manner. *Perhaps I'll manage to survive this day after all*, he thought. But then: "Jennings, Blair . . . and you," he pointed to Stephen, "Blackburn, isn't it?" He motioned to a sturdy-looking cluster of boulders several yards above and to Stephen's right. "Take positions there. Everyone else to the crest!"

Stephen swallowed hard, but hustled to obey the sergeant's command. He realized he'd been placed right in harm's way, with no way to retreat if the position was overrun. But, thankfully, it appeared that anyone attempting to rush these positions was sure to be cut down before they could even get halfway.

Even if there are a thousand of them.

He still had his Sharps carbine, which gave him an advantage over even the infantrymen with whom he'd fallen in. As he and the two other young men settled themselves behind the tall, flat-sided granite rocks, he decided he was in as secure a spot as he could hope for in this place. The rocks surrounded him in a semi-circle, forming a natural breastworks, their upper surfaces irregularly ridged, so that he could easily shoot over the top while presenting only the tiniest of targets.

"I'm Will Jennings," said the fellow to his left, a man of about twenty, with a scraggly beard and pale blue eyes. "Pleased to meetcha."

"And I'm Niles Blair," said the other, an older, dark-haired man with a thin mustache and narrow green eyes. He was already loading his weapon—a British-made Enfield rifle. "Welcome to the 159th."

"Thanks, I'm Stephen Blackburn."

"Cavalry, eh?" asked Blair. "Where's your horse?"

"Shot out from under me."

Jennings whistled. "Rough. We've had a lot of close calls ourselves."

"And I think we're about to have another one," Blair said, staring wide-eyed over the top of the boulders. "Will you just look out there."

Stephen raised his head and looked down the hill.

And wished he hadn't.

Below, to the south and southwest, from the direction of Big Round Top, an ocean of gray was surging forward. He had figured the Union regiments that had just gathered here could easily hold off a thousand. It looked like ten times that number coming their way.

He could already hear the cries of the rebel infantry as they charged. Somewhere above him, he heard Sgt. Craighill calling, "Gentlemen, load your weapons! Prepare to fire!"

"Done!" said Jennings. "We gotta make every shot count!"

Stephen chambered a bullet and slid the bolt home.

He laid his .44 Colt on the rock in front of him, muzzle pointing toward the enemy, ready. His arms trembled.

"Don't shoot too soon," Blair said. "Can't afford to miss. We put enough dead bodies between them and us, their going will be tougher."

Stephen nodded. The now-familiar but still chilling rebel yell rose around him, terrifyingly close. Just above him, he heard Craighill's call of "Rea-dddyyy!"

Jennings slowly raised up, sliding his rifle over the top of the rock. Stephen did the same, hoping their movements would not attract the attention of the leading men in the enemy charge. Blair gave Stephen a supportive pat on the shoulder, and readied his weapon as well.

"Fiiiirrrre!"

There were at least two dozen men only twenty yards away, rushing forward with rifles at the ready. Stephen pulled the trigger and his gun spoke with a loud crack. But it seemed like the world had exploded at the same moment. At once, the men among the rocks fired, as did the lines formed at the top of the hill, and from all points around him. Every man at the front of the rebel advance simply disappeared as a wall of smoke rolled over them like some kind of deadly predator. The men behind them reeled as bodies flew backward, and others stumbled as they found themselves treading on the wreckage of what had only moments before been their comrades in arms.

"Fire at will! Fire at will!"

Stephen chambered another round before the men with the Enfields could even open their powder horns. He aimed into the bodies that quickly replaced the fallen men and squeezed off another round. Blair and Jennings were now tamping their minié balls into the barrels of their muskets. Stephen slid another bullet into the chamber and rose up yet again . . . pulled the trigger . . . and killed another man.

Now, Blair and Jennings were up again. They aimed

quickly, pulled their triggers, and unleashed their own brands of death. The fire coming down on the attackers was withering. Graycoats were falling left and right, bodies rolling back down the hill, tripping the men who kept coming and coming in a never-ending tide. Stephen fired again, his every shot true; this one found its mark in the skull of a young man whose eyes met his only a second before he died.

Stephen shut his mind to it. He had to kill. He had to keep killing them or he was going to die himself. He had never seen so many men converging on a spot in his life.

The hot *zing* of rebel minié balls passing over his head burned his ears, but he could not even think about them. He slid a bullet into the chamber and started to rise up again to shoot. But something suddenly blocked his vision.

A man. A man in a gray coat, swinging the muzzle of his rifle straight toward Stephen.

With a cry, Jennings fell backward, the barrel of his rifle pointing upward. With a deafening *boom* it spewed flame and smoke, and the attacker on the rock whirled and fell out of Stephen's sight. He could only offer Jennings a quick nod of thanks before he heard a scrabbling on the rocks just a couple of feet away. He screamed, knowing what the sound meant. Sliding backward on his buttocks, he hesitated only as long as it took for the head of the attacker to appear over the boulder. Stephen pulled the trigger and the head disappeared.

Blair rose to shoot—and suddenly Stephen felt something hot and wet splash over his face and hands. Glancing sideways, he saw a headless body in a blue uniform standing where Blair had just been. The body toppled—away from Stephen—and he found his mouth gaping in a silent scream, so wide his jaw muscles felt as if they would tear free from his bones. But his fingers somehow found another bullet on his ammunition belt, and shakily inserted it into the smoking chamber. The metal burned his fingers but he barely felt the pain. To his right, several Confederate men rushed around the rocks, but the Federal line up on the hill decimated them before they even saw Stephen and young Jennings.

Stephen crawled over Blair's feet and slid his rifle into a crevice that afforded him a clear shot at a number of men trying to pick their way over the bodies of their comrades. He shot, and a rebel fell clutching his throat. As the man died, his eyes also met Stephen's, as if in accusation. Now it seemed like the dead recognized him. He was no longer just a young man doing his duty. He was a murderer. Many times over.

I have to kill them or I am a dead man.

They had killed Blair. They had killed Col. Hawkins, and Sgt. Mansfield. They had probably killed Marshall. In his heart, Stephen felt he would never see his best friend ever again. They deserved to die.

And they think the same of me!

"Oh, Christ," he whispered, his hands barely able to hold the rifle. Tears rimmed his eyes and he shook them away. His energy had all but departed.

But the enemy paid his weakness no mind. They kept coming, and the men in blue kept firing, wiping out line after line of the attackers. Yet no matter how many fell, more kept coming, their yells of fury drowning out even the gunfire. Next to him, Jennings shouted, "Looks like a bloody slaughter pen down there!" He rose and fired off a shot, taking down a man. But before he could duck back down behind his cover of rocks, a minié ball ripped into his shoulder, and with a cry of shock, he whirled backward, striking Stephen and knocking him off-balance.

Jennings rolled away from him, moaning in agony, the sound so pitiable that Stephen felt new tears burning in his eyes. His rifle felt like it weighed two tons as he tried to struggle back onto his knees. He could hear the thudding of footsteps just on the other side of the rocks. He raised his rifle, knowing that at any second the man on the other side would come into view. He would have to kill again or he would die. This ugly, rocky ground was not where he wanted to die.

A silhouette appeared atop the rocks and Stephen's finger tightened on the trigger. What he didn't expect was for three more figures to materialize instantaneously alongside the first. His mouth fell open in surprise at the same time his rifle spoke. The first man lurched and fell backward, disappearing from his view. But he could not reload in time to repel the others. With a yell as fierce as that of the Rebels themselves, he raised his rifle to use it like a club, to simply beat his attackers away. With all his energy, he swung.

But the rifle slipped from his grasp and went flying through the air, barely missing the head of one of the rebels. For a moment, Stephen did not realize why he had lost his grip. It seemed that many silent seconds passed before he heard the deafening boom of the shot and felt an impact beneath his right collarbone that took his breathe away. He found himself gazing into a pair of pale blue eyes that looked curiously back at him before a cloud of smoke rolled between them, completely obscuring his vision.

And then his knees simply buckled beneath him and he collapsed like a satchel of clay bricks. His head struck the hard earth with a sickening thud, and in that moment, he saw a streamer of blood arcing skyward as if in slow motion, and it wasn't until the world began to go dark around him that he realized, horribly, without any doubt, that that blood came from a gaping hole in his own body.

23

SHE STOOD INSIDE the doorway of Christ Lutheran Church, and could move no farther.

The sanctuary before her was filled with gnarled, torn, and mangled bodies on pews, on the aisle floor, on stretchers and blankets. Some lay on makeshift tables constructed of boards across barrel tops. Lanterns burned from walls and altar candles, and a semblance of light filtered through the windows along the sides. The place hung thick with the smell of blood and sweat and agony.

But the sounds were the worst.

Moans. Screams. Nurses talking in whispers that were most often drowned out by the cries of the pitiable soldiers in their pitiable conditions. Men calling for Jesus, for their mothers, for their wives and sweethearts. Surgeons calling to each other for help in removing men who had died.

Stephen cannot be in here! Susanne put her hand to her mouth, wishing for once to be wearing gloves that might help mask the stench. *Yet I must look. I have to see for myself.*

God, give me strength!

From outside, the sound of the battle thundered from the south.

"Thank you for coming!" said a middle-aged woman in a white apron and white scarf covering her hair. She hurried up the church's aisle, stepping around and over men on the floor, and put her hand on Susanne's shoulder. "We thought we'd see no more nurses today! God bless you, dear!" Close now, Susanne could see her apron was smeared in blood.

"Oh, no," said Susanne. "I'm not a nurse. I'm here to find my brother."

"I'm not a nurse, either," said the woman. "I am a teacher at our girl's school. But today I am a nurse. As are all able-bodied and charitable women."

"I want to find my brother."

"His name?"

It was hard to speak his name in such a place. "Stephen," said Susanne. "Blackburn."

The nurse smiled gently and shook her head. "I've not heard that name spoken here."

To the right, amid the hubbub and cries, two surgeons had straddled a man on a pew. One held a scalpel aloft. The man's pant leg was torn away, exposing the shattered calf, with the foot braced on top of a barrel. Around the leg just above the knee was a tourniquet. A nurse was holding the man's head. In the man's mouth was a rag soaked in some sort of fluid. His eyes rolled in the sockets and he groaned into the rag.

In a move so brutal yet clean, the man with the large scalpel brought the blade down and into the flesh of the leg at the knee. He drew it around the whole of the leg. The skin and muscle opened, parting at the scalpel's bite. Blood poured, scarlet and thick, drenching the surgeon's hand. The man on the pew twisted his head and gagged around the rag. His eyes fluttered open, then shut. The nurse said, "It will be over soon!"

"Praise God we've a bit of chloroform," said the nurse to Susanne. "The first ones wounded are more lucky than the next to come. We are low on supplies already. There will be many men who will suffer amputation without the help of anesthesia."

The surgeon dropped the scalpel and was handed a hacksaw. He leaned in and began to saw quickly into the bone below the gaping flesh. Susanne spun away, unable to watch more. Bits of undigested venison from the previous night's supper rushed into her throat, her mouth, and she bent over to spit them out.

"It is not a pretty sight," said the nurse. "But we haven't time to worry about pretty. Many men will lose limbs today. Minié balls shatter bone, and bone so destroyed will never heal. If the surgery is done within the first twenty-four hours of the injury, a man will likely survive. If we wait much longer, the chance that he will die grows greatly."

Susanne drew herself back up and wiped her mouth. "I . . . must find my brother."

"I would not begin to know how to help you," said the nurse. "It would be a waste of time, and we have so little time as you can see." She swept her arm outward, indicating all the men in the room. "They will all die if we do not help them. And quickly!"

"May I look?"

"Look? Can't you stay and help? We need extra hands, and you look strong and courageous."

"I . . . no. I have to find Stephen. I need to know if he is among the wounded . . ."

"Or among the dead?" came another voice from behind. Susanne looked around to find a young man standing against the wall near the door, dressed in civilian clothing and holding a pad of paper in his hand. He wore no hat, and his sandy brown hair was matted to his head. His eyes were blue.

"And sir," said Susanne irritably. "Who asked you to join our conversation? This is a personal matter!"

"I beg your pardon, Miss," he said. "I've been here

several hours, and I'm afraid all this inhumanity has affected my attitude."

The nurse excused herself and hastened back up the aisle. To either side of the sanctuary, Susanne saw that a good many other men were being prepared for amputation. Nurses were tying tourniquets around arms and legs and ankles. The men, not yet drugged, squirmed and prayed for what was soon to happen to them. Susanne noticed that not far from her beside the baptismal font were several large baskets. They were filled with dismembered arms and legs. She began to shake.

None of this is possible!

"My name is Tristan Gordon," said the young man. "I am a sketch artist and reporter for a newspaper in Philadelphia."

Susanne looked at the man but could not speak. How could he speak so casually in such a terrible yet sacred place?

He took several steps forward. "And you are?"

Susanne felt her chest heaving uncontrollably, and suddenly, she was sobbing. She held her waist and drove her chin to her chest, trying to stop, but she could not. The tears were hot and furious and insistent. "It . . . doesn't matter who I am!" she managed. "Will . . . you . . . help me look or not? His name is Stephen Blackburn. He is sixteen, with auburn hair, the color of mine."

The man's face softened. He held out his free hand for a moment as if trying to comfort her. Then the hand dropped to his side. "I'm sorry, Miss. I know this place is beyond description, which is why I must come and draw what I see for the readers back home. They must know the truth. I have followed battles for over a year, and I, too, wept at first."

"You no longer care?" Susanne looked up accusingly.

"I cry my tears in private now," he said. "I've found it is easier on the dying to see a hopeful face rather than one torn with guilt, fear, or anger, or sorrow."

Susanne drove the heels of her hands into her eyes, and the weeping slowed. She shuddered, wiped her nose, and sniffed. "Perhaps you are right," she said. "I can do no one any good making such a scene."

"Yet it is understandable," said Tristan.

"No matter," said Susanne. "Will you help me? Or just stand there and draw for your newspaper?"

"I shall help you," Tristan said. "We can both ask, and cover more ground more quickly."

"Thank you, Mr. Gordon."

"Tristan," he said.

"Tristan, then."

He nodded, and, tucking his pad of paper inside his shirt, moved off to the right side of the sanctuary. He began bending over each man as he passed, whispering a question, and then moving on. Susanne watched him for a moment, then did the same, moving to the left side of the large room. The first few men were on the floor, on bedrolls no thicker than several sheets. One had his jaw bandaged, the second was sitting with his arm in a sling. The third seemed either unconscious or dead.

"Hello, ma'am," said the man with the sling. He had an accent not of Pennsylvania, but of somewhere much father north. "Bless you for your kindness."

"Oh, I'm not . . . ," Susanne began, but the look in the man's eyes told her that it might be of comfort to him to believe yet another nurse had arrived to assist. And so she merely said, "Thank you, sir. You have done our country a great service."

The man smiled and nodded. "I hope our boys make their stand out there."

"As do I," said Susanne. "Do you know Stephen Blackburn?"

"No, ma'am, can't say I do."

Susanne moved on to the next two men. A nurse was tending the first, holding his hand and wiping his brow with a wet cloth. His arm was gone from the elbow, and recently so, as he was dazed and just coming around from the chloroform. The nurse smiled up at Susanne and said, "I'm so glad you've come. We are so short-handed. If you have any questions, just ask. I am trained as a nurse, and can help get you started."

Susanne said nothing, and moved to the next man. This one had burns on his chest, and blood and pus had seeped through the thin bandages. "Miss," he said, "my arms are hurting might bad, but these bandages are drawing flies. Could you change them for me? I'd do it if I could."

Susanne hesitated, then said, "Of course, sir." Gently she took the edge of the bandage with her fingers and peeled it away from the man's chest. Strips of flesh came off with it, and it began to bleed anew. The man grit his teeth and drew a sharp breath, but made no other sound. The nurse next to Susanne pointed to a dwindling stack of bandages near the window. Susanne unfolded the largest one she could find and lay it across the burned chest. "I don't know what else . . . ," she began, but the man closed his eyes and through tight jaws said, "Better, that's better."

Susanne swallowed, but her throat was dry.

The next man was lying on a pew. He was thin, with black hair and a spattering of a beard along his jawline. He looked young, but Susanne couldn't tell, for most of his face, save his mouth, was blown off. She prayed the man was not conscious, or was dead, for no one could endure such a fate. But as she began to pass him by, he spoke. "Nurse?"

Susanne turned back, startled that he could speak, and horrified that he was awake and aware. "Yes?" she managed.

"What day is it?" The words were drawled out with the effects of drugs—morphine, she guessed.

"It is July 2, sir."

"Sir? I'm only fifteen."

"Oh," said Susanne. What could she say? She couldn't tell him it would be all right, for it wouldn't.

Nothing this side of heaven could make this poor boy all right.

"I have to talk to a priest," said the boy. "Is there one here?"

"No," said Susanne, glancing about. There seemed to be no priest, no chaplain. Clearly, the war had well outgrown the local supply of the ministry. They were elsewhere, she was certain, but at this moment, not inside this church.

"Oh!" said the boy. His voice twisted, suddenly full of fear and anguish. "No priest!"

Susanne thought it sounded ridiculous as she spoke, but she found herself saying, "I'm the daughter of a minister."

"Catholic?"

"Lutheran."

"Is that Christian?"

"Yes."

"Would you hear my confession?"

"Can I do that?"

"God did not see fit to have a priest here," said the boy, his voice a labored whisper. "But he brought a minister's daughter."

Susanne looked up, hoping a nurse nearby might see her predicament and come to her aid. But everyone had their hands full. At least three amputations were going on that she could see. Other men were writhing with nurses trying to calm and tend them. She could no longer even see Tristan. Maybe he'd given up looking for Stephen and had left.

"Nurse?"

Susanne looked down at the boy. He wasn't Stephen, but dearest God, he might have a sister somewhere who was looking for him, too. She pushed up her sleeves, knowing the boy could not see her disfigured arms and then deeply ashamed that she would even care about her arms now, and took his hand in hers. "All right," she said. "I'm here. I'm listening."

The boy was weak, and his words slow and thick on his tongue. "First of all, I did not read my Bible this morning. Ah, my poor mother and father, that I did not, for I shall never be able to read it again."

Tears sprang afresh to Susanne's eyes, but she kept the tears from her voice. "Yes, go on."

"I cussed in the Lord's name. I cheated at dice last night." He paused, and took a long, rasping breath though his mouth. "I . . . I forgot to write my mother, and now look at me. I look dreadful, don't I? I will scare her when she sees me, won't I?"

Susanne felt her face sting with sorrow. "You . . . you are wounded, but you will never frighten your mother. She loves you."

The boy said, "My mother loves me, oh, that is true."

"It is."

"Will you stay a while?"

"I will."

The boy went silent then. Susanne held his hand and squeezed it as easily as she could.

"Sleep," she said. "Sleep, and have beautiful dreams."

She sat there for a long time. The light through the windows shifted, indicating the day was growing longer. Her arm grew tired, holding the boy's hand, but she would not let go.

Sometime later, a nurse was standing at her side, and saying, "Honey, he's done in. He's gone."

Startled, Susanne looked up. She felt she'd been in a trance. "What did you say?"

The nurse who had met her when she'd first arrive said, "He's passed on. We need to move him, for more wounded are coming in. More ambulances are arriving from the battlefield."

Susanne stood on shaky legs. She rubbed her arms, trying to bring back circulation. Then she looked up to see Tristan watching her from close by.

"Did you . . . ?" she asked.

"No, no Stephen Blackburn," he said. "I'm terribly sorry."

"Should I praise God for that?" she asked wearily. "Or be angry? Perhaps he is not wounded, but riding about waving that sabre he'd always dreamed about, finding his glory."

"Perhaps," said Tristan. He said, "Where do you live? I should be honored to walk you home. Reporters, surgeons, and nurses are pretty much left alone. We are known as no threat. We're considered neutrals."

"I live quite far," said Susanne. She moved out of the front door to the steps of the church. Tristan followed. In front of the church, several two-wheeled ambulances had arrived with their dreadful cargo, and groaning, bleeding men were being unloaded on stretchers. She went down the steps to see if any of the new arrivals were Stephen. They were not. "I have a horse, somewhere," she said to Tristan. "The Alms House, if the Rebels haven't spotted her by now and stolen her away."

"Shall I walk you to the Alms House to have a look?"

"I do not want to inconvenience you."

"You are too kind and too lovely to be an inconvenience."

Susanne started, and stared at Tristan. Lovely? Was he making fun of her? Quickly she pulled down her sleeves. Surely he'd seen the burns. Uncle Silas had said she was plain. She'd never thought of herself as anything but plain.

But the look in Tristan's eyes revealed something else. Something true and honest, something open and kind. She said, "I . . . I don't know what you mean."

Tristan held up the pad of paper, and carefully tore off the top sheet. He handed it to Susanne. "I am paid to show the truth. The battles, when I can find a place to hide in the trees or brush. The injured, when I can get inside a field hospital. And anything else that completes the story. I drew you as you tended the boy. As you sat and held his hand and gave him the tenderness he needed in those last moments. I have never seen such beauty."

Susanne looked at the paper. It was a sketch, finely detailed and finely executed. It showed a beautiful young woman seated beside a boy with no face, bending down, her face alight with concern and compassion.

"I do not know your name," said Tristan. His voice was pinched but steady. She wondered if he were on the verge of tears, himself. "But you do not need to tell me. You've given me a gift today, one I shall never forget."

Susanne looked at the sketch and then looked at Tristan. "My name is Susanne Blackburn," she whispered.

"Susanne," he said.

She nodded.

"May I write to you?" He sounded hopeful. "Sometime? I am on the road a lot with the war. But sometime?"

Slowly, Susanne nodded. "I receive my letters in Gettysburg."

"Susanne!" The voice was loud and near. Susanne spun about, and there was Aunt Rudine pounding up the street, her wide hooped skirt bouncing back and forth.

"It's my aunt!" Susanne said incredulously. She tucked the drawing into her pocket with her journal, and watched as the woman approached, her face shaded beneath her wide-brimmed, flower-studded bonnet. As Aunt Rudine drew close to Susanne, her hands went out, and Susanne prepared to be clouted on the ears. She stepped back.

But Aunt Rudine grabbed Susanne in a rough hug and drew her in close. Susanne gasped, but did not pull away. The woman who prided herself on decorum and delicacy, was sweating and filthy and disheveled. But after the barest moment, Aunt Rudine herself pushed away, and pointed a gloved finger at Susanne's face.

"How dare you run off from me! How dare you! I cannot . . . I will not . . . lose anymore family members! Do you hear me?"

Susanne said, "Aunt Rudine . . ."

"Do you *hear* me? I had to ride Simon's pony clear from Sycamore Grove to find you! I had the pony stolen out from under me by some renegades on Baltimore Street! I had to tell every Reb I met that I had consumption, *consumption,* of all things, so I would be left alone! There is fighting going on as we speak, can you not hear the gunfire south of us? And here I am, alone, facing danger, trying to find you and bring you home!"

"Aunt Rudine, I'm all right. I'm safe. I want to find Stephen. I don't want to lose him, either!"

But the woman continued. Her proper demeanor had collapsed, and her voice spiraled upward. "Can you not hear the cries of those men in the churches? Can you not hear them dying?" Her hands went over her ears. "Can you?"

"Yes."

"Then can you not understand—" And Rudine, who had never been anything but harsh and cruel, put her dirty gloves over her eyes and began to cry. "Can you not understand that I will not allow my family to be torn to pieces? I will not allow Simon to be harmed! I will not allow my mother to lose her mind and be gone to us! I will not allow you to run off. Stephen took it upon himself to go. My husband took it upon himself to—" She stomped her foot. She began to cry.

"To what?"

Her face, streaked with anger, was raised to meet Susanne's. "To run off and leave us. To find another woman, a *hussy,* and leave us for her! To take most of our money, all of our servants, and the remainder of my pride. He did not join the army, curse him, he joined with a harlot! But I shall lose no more. I will not allow it!"

Susanne looked back toward the church. Tristan Gordon was gone. She closed her eyes slowly, and took a breath. Then, turning again to Aunt Rudine, she said, "I'm sorry about your husband. But as Stephen left to become a man, you must allow me to become a woman. I am no longer a child."

"No more words!" snapped the woman. She touched her face with her hands to remove the tears and lifted her chin haughtily. "I've had my say. Isn't that what you think everyone should do? Tell their secrets? Well, I've told you mine, and nothing is better for it. Nothing is changed. And you shall never speak of it again. Now, come with me. We shall return to the farm."

"The nurse and the woman with consumption," said Susanne.

"You shall not make sport!"

"I am not going home until I find my brother."

"And I shall not go back without you."

"Please yourself," said Susanne. "I've searched but one church, and there are a dozen more to go."

Aunt Rudine fell into a furious silence. She walked with Susanne toward Baltimore Street, her head held high. "It would be best if you were to cough on occasion," said Susanne, but Aunt Rudine said nothing. The sound of cannons and guns continued on the outskirts of town, and uniformed rebels raced back and forth along the street. "Consumption!" Susanne shouted, "I am a nurse!" as four Confederates on horseback slowed their mounts in front of them on the road. Aunt Rudine cringed, but then coughed, and the soldiers steered clear.

They paused at the street corner as another four horse-drawn ambulances rattled by. Susanne called out, "Stephen?" but there was no answer. She ran up beside one of them and tried to keep pace, and peered inside the open sides. Road grit sprayed her face.

She did not know these men.

The visited Saint Francis Xavier Church and the Common School, the Presbyterian Church and the

German Reformed Church, where more torn and bloodied men had been brought to tend. Aunt Rudine refused to go inside. Susanne went in alone. But Stephen was not there.

The sun was low in the west now, and shadows hung long and black over the streets and yards.

"What do you propose to do now, young lady?" demanded Aunt Rudine. "Come nightfall the cry of consumption will have little effect on rebels drunk on ale and whiskey!"

"Indeed," said Susanne. Her head ached dreadfully from weariness and heartbreak. Where was Stephen? "We should find a place to sleep and begin again tomorrow."

"Sleep where, young lady?"

"I don't care!" cried Susanne. "In a shed, in a pig stye, somewhere!"

"No need to be rude," said Aunt Rudine.

They walked up Baltimore Street. Susanne knew many families were still in town, but many would be hiding in their cellars and attics and would never open their doors to a knock. Other homes were occupied by the enemy. The sounds of gunfire in the distance ceased. The day's fighting was done. Sounds of music began to take it's place as the occupying soldiers made ready for a night's relaxation.

They reached the front of the courthouse. "This is where he signed up," said Susanne. "This is where he left us." She bit her lip firmly. Crying would do no good.

Inside the courthouse came the familiar cries of suffering humanity. Lanterns burned brightly from within. This hospital, as the others, would likely be working without stop. A man came outside with a crate load of arms and legs and put them in the grass near a line of wounded men who, on stretchers, had yet to be moved inside. Susanne said, "We best go in. I can think of no other place we shall be safe."

"I cannot go in with that carnage!"

"They are men!" said Susanne. "They are living, breathing flesh and blood! They are Stephen! They are Marshall! They are Simon and Uncle Silas and even your husband! Good and bad, smart and dull, but they are men who have given themselves for us. They are not ghosts nor demons!"

"Be quiet, child!"

And Susanne, in her rage, stepped forward to strike her aunt, to slap away the arrogance and the cold-heartedness. To drive some sense into the otherwise petty mind and shallow heart.

But as she swung her arm out she tripped over a bloodied man on a stretcher on the ground.

"Oh!" she cried, flailing her hands to keep her balance. But she lost it, and crashed to her knees, barely missing the man as she fell. "Oh, dear!" she gasped. "Sir, I am sorry. I gave you a fright. That is the last thing I meant to do!"

The man mumbled something incoherent and kicked out with his foot as if spurring a horse onward in a troubled dream. Susanne sat up and looked at him. He was in dire shape, his shoulder crushed by a minié ball and drenched in red.

Another one, God bless him.

He was not very old, with auburn hair and a beard. He . . .

"Sweet Jesus!" whispered Susanne. Her heart stopped. It held. It began beating again.

"Don't take the Lord's name in vain," said Aunt Rudine.

But Susanne was beyond hearing any words her aunt said, because her heart was leaping and trembling with joy. She took the young man's hand in hers, held it to her cheek, and raised her grateful voice to the sky. "Stephen! Thank God! Thank God!"

24

July 12, 1863

I can't believe I'm alive.

I don't remember much of the last few days, and if Susanne hadn't told me, I wouldn't know what today is. It hurts even to hold a pen and paper, but I want to say what I have to say while I'm awake. I've been asleep a lot, and they tell me I lost a huge amount of blood. They got the ball out of me at the courthouse hospital. I hear it came real close to my lung. Another half inch and it would probably have killed me on the spot. It's probably a good thing I got shot point blank though because they left me for dead right then and there. If it hadn't been for that, they'd probably have put more holes in me just to make sure. Still, it mangled my shoulder real bad, and it hurts all the way around to my back and sometimes as far down as my feet.

I haven't ever known what pain was up until now. I've been through the worst days and nights I've ever known. They got me home, and I'm here in my own bed, and something about it just doesn't seem real. It's only been a couple of months I've been gone from here, but somehow the army life seems the most real thing I've ever known.

Susanne is very happy to have me back. Uncle Silas has been his usual irritable self, but seems to be keeping his complaints to a low growl. Susanne tells me Simon often comes in to sit with me while I'm asleep. Aunt Darcy, I understand, who had lost even more of her mind a short while ago is coming around, and every so often I see her peer into my room with a look of pure joy on her face. Aunt Rudine, however, has little sympathy for what I've been through.

Still it's good to be home. Believe it or not, I care about them. All of them. This is my family, such as it is.

Susanne has kept my wound cleaned and freshly dressed, and she gives me whiskey to help the pain when she knows nobody else is around. She tells me the men that brought me home from town left a bottle for me, and Mr. Bowler has sent a couple, too. I don't reckon under the circumstances the family would really care, but right now I don't want anyone to take it away from me. There's times it hurts so bad there's nothing else that helps.

I heard Jennie Wade got killed. The only civilian in the whole of Gettysburg to die, shot dead in her sister's kitchen while making bread. I cannot imagine never seeing her face on the walks and in the shops again.

And as I was afraid, Marshall's gone. He just disappeared from the face of the earth. I know he got slaughtered that day I just barely got away from the rebel charge. I guess I knew it all along, and I've tried not to think about it. Now I'm here, and I'm not having to fight to save my own skin from rebel guns, I've had time to deal with it. Corporal Jennings was right—it's a hard thing to have a friend in battle. Because it can rip your heart right out. When it's your friend that's killed, it's really a part of you.

Sometimes the gunshot wound is easier to bear.

His poor family. His parents haven't come to see me yet. I reckon they will when they feel like they're strong enough to see me. The boy that lived when theirs died.

I don't know if I'll ever heal enough to go back to the army, but I want to. I may have gone off because it seemed like the best way out of here, but I believe it was the right thing to do. It'll be a long time before I'll be able to hold a rifle. But some day. Maybe it's because going back will help make Marshall's sacrifice mean something, at least to me personally.

After all's said and done it looks like General Lee and the Rebels got run back to Virginia. I wouldn't say our side really won the day, though, either. The newspapers report that the losses our army took were truly horrendous. Gen. Meade took a bad beating for the first couple of days, and he knows it. But after we've come through such a battle, I wonder if there could ever be another one like it. That was the best the Rebels had to throw at us, and now they're back on the defensive. One of the men that brought me back said it's just a matter of time now. The Union's going to chase Lee until he's backed into a corner and he's got no choice but to give up.

I just wonder how many more lives that's going to cost.

I guess now I'm going to have a duty here at home. Susanne's told me about what she's gone through while I was away. Makes me sometimes feel bad for leaving, but I can't dwell on that. I guess what I can do now is try to make peace in whatever small way I can for this family. If we're not able to work things out in our own little Union, how can anybody ever succeed in a big one? We have to start somewhere.

I'm hurting from sitting up, so I guess I'm going to try to get some more sleep. I got half a bottle left under the bed, I guess I'll knock down a few slugs to take the edge off the pain, enough to relax a bit.

I can hear them down in the kitchen, I guess they're

going to be cooking dinner soon. It's such a normal sound, and I think I'm truly glad to hear it. There's a lot of men not lucky enough to be hearing anything like that ever again. Marshall Fenwick won't ever know that little joy, or any other. I guess every man that died was somebody's friend. Somebody's family.

I thought maybe I'd done all my crying. But maybe not. I think I got to stop writing now, because I'm hurting real bad. Not just the wound.

I'll be damned. I didn't know Susanne was outside my door. She must have heard me. Because now she's crying too.

END